# Walk In

**by**

**Kate Spencer**

Published by

The Lightworkers Academy

Printed by Lightning Source, Milton Keynes, UK

## Dedication

To all of the square pegs and odd sockers of the world.

If you are lucky enough to be different, don't ever change.

# Prologue

I could see you through the whispery veil that separates the worlds.

You sat in the dark with your knees hugged up to your chest and your heart shattered into a million shards of misery.

All cried out.

You rocked back and forth and a soft, breathy plea escaped from your lips as you closed your eyes tight.

"Help me, please someone help me."

I reached through the veil to touch you and send you thoughts of love and comfort, but desperation and alcohol had numbed you to anything other than the pain that coiled around you, constricting more and more. I stroked your cheek and whispered words of courage, but they couldn't reach you through your foggy desperation.

Asking now for a full connection, I held my nerve. This was something we rarely do as we receive all thoughts and feelings in a single moment. With no filters this can overwhelm us, and we can lose our objectivity. I had to stay focused.

Your vortex of your emotion started dragging me down into the abyss that you had fought for so long, and I caught my breath. I knew that this would have to happen now.

"Please help me, someone h-h-help me," you stammered again, and I gave permission for The Exchange.

Your thoughts showed that we only had moments left before you made the decision. You had calmly popped pills from silver foil wrappers, and thrown them all together into a pink and white candy striped paper bag. A deadly pick-and-mix.

I needed a healthy body and intelligent brain, and among all of the candidates that I had considered, you were the most compatible. I couldn't let you do this now.

I asked that the veil be lowered in order for the process to start, and I reached out to you again. I knelt now and cupped your face, as you looked at me in wonder. You rubbed your eyes and blinked them wide open, shaking your head as your lips parted but no words were spoken.

I kissed your forehead, and gently my thumbs skimmed your under-eyes and caught the tears that had not yet fallen.

"Hello," I spoke softly to you and you blinked again, shaking your head from side to side.

"I am here from another time and space and I have been watching over you," I continued. "I know that you are unhappy with your life here on Earth."

Your head bowed and I heard more tears catch in your throat, as I folded my arms and wings around your shivery body. I could feel the pain from your heart pouring into me with every passing moment; I knew that this had to be fast.

"Who are you?" you whispered.

"I am here to offer you a different life, a chance to start over and be happy, to leave behind these hard lessons and to go back home."

"Home?" you asked.

"Yes, Home." I projected the picture now and as you watched it flicker to life, I felt your soul connect. The image looked like the Earth, but in her most radiant moments, and magnified. Every blade of grass that covered rolling hills was vividly green and lush, and the blossoms on the trees were soft shades of pink and lilac as they danced in a warm breeze. Water flowed in a stream that tumbled into ice blue pools where azure dragonflies hovered, and love radiated like a heartbeat. The magnetic pull of familiarity started to melt away your resistance.

"I remember," you said, smiling and nodding as the reflection danced in your eyes. You reached out to touch the image, but in physical form your fingers only rippled the surface.

"This is why I have come to you," I said, "to exchange."

You took a deep breath and looked through the translucent image, soaking up the reality of the room we were in now. It hinted at the bigger picture of your life, mismatched and disheveled bedding, a curtain rail hanging on by one screw, threadbare carpet and a pile of dirty washing. The television blared downstairs, gunfire and sirens.

You laughed and shook your head.

"And you want this?" you asked me. "And him?"

"I'm on a mission," I answered you and smiled, "I have my reasons."

"I can't say I understand why, but if you want to exchange that's fine by me. You're welcome to my life, if you can call it that," you said, and looked at me with your head on one side and sighed, "Whoever you are."

We both nodded and the intention was activated.

I felt the merging begin.

Your soul started to vibrate at a higher frequency as your skin began to glow and pixelate into moving particles of light. Your eyes blazed indigo and all traces of pain dissolved in their beauty, I could feel your heart expanding with the love and connection to all that is. Your energy started to swirl out of your body and towards those waiting for you. At first it looked like thin silver tendrils, but as they started to weave and entwine, their creative intelligence drew together the filaments of your soul, and there you were in all of your radiance.

You stepped across the rainbow bridge that connects dimensions and for a second or two the body was empty, hollow. You smiled over your shoulder and waved at me, you were moving in and out of

3

the familiar form that was your physical appearance on Earth, a hologram walking between the worlds. I smiled back as your wings unfolded behind you.

"It's time," I heard clearly.

The part of me that was still at Home felt my soul group surround me now. They wished me well on my mission, and reminded me that time passes much more slowly on Earth. To them I would be gone for a few weeks, but to me it would literally be a lifetime.

I stepped forwards and dipped one foot into the clear membrane, knowing that the pool of forgetfulness would banish my soul memories into the depths of my subconscious mind. This was part of the agreement. I looked back and smiled. "Be sure to watch over me," I said as I tiptoed tentatively. AJ was sending me thought forms of encouragement and love, saying that we would be back together soon. Our signatures were very alike; to humans this energy is known as twin flame or soul mate. I felt a wave of emotion as I was submerged momentarily, and then spiraled down towards the Earth plane. He called to me as I flew weightlessly through dimensions and his words rang out as I juddered into the body of Amelia Grace Brown.

"I'll find you," echoed through my senses, as I sat shell-shocked, wondering what could possibly be going on.

I blinked my eyes and tried to adjust to the surroundings, my head was swimming and I fought back vomit. I had watched humans for long enough to know that this was due to the volume of alcohol that Amelia had consumed that night, and that I would feel worse tomorrow. I dragged my heavy body to the bed and kneeled. My hands folded together and I prayed that this would pass. I was emotionally and intellectually strong, but I couldn't function in a physical world if it felt like this. I waited a moment for the nausea to subside, then heaved myself onto the mattress.

A weird combination of memories and experiences flashed through my mind, some vivid and some vague, I couldn't distinguish what was real and not, there seemed to be no timeline. I surrendered and allowed sleep to take me even deeper, a part of me thought that this might be The Integration. It happens quickly after The Exchange and often in sleep state. I saw flashes of different incarnations and the lives of humans I had overlooked in preparation to come to Earth. These screen shots were sometimes stills and sometimes like movies, and in one or two that were very emotionally charged I was able to participate rather than observe.

I had heard that you get some access to the memories of the first inhabitant of your body; these are energetically coded into cell memory. This would be useful when I had to start interacting with people in my life, to pick up the thread of who they were and how they fitted into my world. I recognized faces and feelings because of the work that I had done in overlooking Amelia before The Exchange, but this process was more than that. It was like weaving together the threads of consciousness, one life into another. My soul was plaiting tiny cords of emotion, relationship, experience and memory so tightly that they became one seamless fabric of knowing.

I could feel my limbs twitching slightly and my eyelids flicker as more and more information was downloaded and encoded. I sent messages to the physical body to relax and allow.

# Chapter 1

A mile and a half away, the second hand swept past midnight in the darkness of the forest, the flickering orange glow from the campfire illuminated the time.

"That's it then." Orin's voice was strong and controlled, but his body language betrayed this. He sighed and clasped his hands together before raising his head and making eye contact with the two others.

"If the prophecy is right, today is the day that she will come."

They nodded in agreement and the girl spoke up. "Maybe we should try one more time?"

Orin shook his head. "Emma you know it won't work with just the three of us."

The girl pulled her coat around her tighter as the moon shone a shaft of white light through a gap in the trees and into the clearing.

"Look Orin," she half smiled and spoke softly now, casting her eyes upwards, "maybe it's a sign?"

Orin shook his head and sighed again. "Blue, help me out here."

The third member of the circle shrugged his shoulders and his eyes stayed fixed on the dancing flames. "I don't know."

Emma stood up and hugged her arms around herself, stamped her feet a couple of times and made her way to the circular patch of dead leaves on the forest floor. Her breath puffed out white clouds and an owl hooted in the distance, small twigs snapped with each step.

"I just want to see it at least." She raised her right arm to waist height, palm pointing downward.

At first there was a gentle rustling of the leaves, as the wind made them dance in a swirling waltz at her feet. Both her concentration and the tempo increased as she moved them faster and faster, until soon the moon shone like a spotlight on a tornado of browns, reds and yellows that was the same height as the girl that controlled it. She moved her hand to the right carefully, and the funnel of leaves moved with it, then she pointed to the ground and they fell quietly into a neat pile.

"Good practice!" she said and turned her attention to the stone circle that had been revealed. The other two stood now and joined her; they could clearly see the four points of the compass that had been carved into the ancient grey slab.

Each of them knew their position from the book. Their feet had to touch but not their hands, their hands were to receive. They knew as well that without the fourth member that they would not be able to fully activate either this inter-dimensional portal or their own abilities. Although they could use them now, it was in a diluted form.

It had taken them what seemed like an age to find each other, and they had come together through a series of strange coincidences or maybe destiny. For the last three years though, all they had been searching for was her. They didn't know where she would come from or what she would look like, all they knew was that there would be a knowing, a recognition, just like there was when they found one another.

It was prophesied that after today their chance would be lost.

"She just has to come today," Emma said and shivered as a cloud covered the moon and the dark grew darker.

"We've got to believe that," Orin spoke in a serious tone. "Or who knows what will happen."

"We all know what will happen," said Blue solemnly.

"That's why Emma's right, she has to come today."

Emma reached out her hand again and moved the leaves back over the stone circle, and the fire started to smolder. "We'd better get back before our folks know we're gone," she said. "Blue?"

He paused for a moment and closed his eyes. "It's all good. But your brother is getting up for a glass of water just after you get back."

"Let's split." Orin stamped out the last of the embers and the three made their way up through the familiar track towards the sleeping town.

"Can't you see her Blue?" asked Emma in a whisper. "I mean if she's coming today you would see her?"

"I can't. I've tried loads of times and for some reason I'm blocked," he replied.

"It's a lesson in faith," said Orin. "We have to know and believe that she is coming in order to allow it to happen, you need to stop being so scared that it won't, Emma."

"Get out of my head!" hissed Emma playfully. "You space invader!"

"Stop thinking so loud then!" Orin chuckled and playfully ruffled her hair.

They crossed the deserted road now and walked quickly onto the outskirts of a housing estate.

"Five minutes... he's stirring," Blue reminded her, and she turned to run quietly down the driveway to her home, blowing them both silent kisses.

Orin turned to Blue and spoke in a serious tone, "I know what you can see."

"I can't help it. I see likely future possibilities and that *is* a possibility at the moment, it's out there and it could happen." Blue stopped walking and faced Orin. "I get flashes of it working out as well you know, but less than I used to. It's like the closer something gets the more clearly I can see the most likely outcome. The other outcomes are there, but just becoming less possible I guess." Blue shrugged and sighed at the seriousness of the situation.

"I didn't mean to be hard on you, I know that you can't control it. Maybe Emma's right and I should stop being such a space invader!" Orin laughed and play-punched his friend in the arm, who punched him back.

"She will come," Orin said as he composed himself.

"Maybe she's been under our noses all of the time and we just haven't recognized her," said Blue.

"Maybe." Orin laughed and ran his fingers through his hair. "Who knows, maybe she'll show up at school tomorrow."

Blue replied sarcastically, "Yeah, I can see it now, she'll arrive wearing a cape and use her superpowers to break down the doors and shout 'anyone missing North?'"

Orin played along. "Totally, I see it now! She's wondering what all the fuss was about, she was always going to get here on time!"

"Women!" replied Blue and shook his head.

"Speaking of women… you do *know* that Emma likes you, don't you?" Orin smiled.

"Course she likes me, we're a team," shrugged Blue. "I like her as well."

"No I mean she *likes* you!"

Orin waited for a response and his loaded statement hung in the air between them for a second as the penny dropped.

"No way… I mean, like *that*?" Blue's eyebrows arched in surprise. "How do you know?"

"What do you mean how do I know? I've heard in detail what she wants to do with you…" Orin laughed and made his way towards home.

As Orin turned to wave he saw the silhouette of his friend punching the night air in victory and heard his thoughts shout, "Yes!" He smiled to himself, he had known for a long time that they would be good for each other, but had to try to let them find out for themselves. Nothing wrong with planting the seed, and anyway Blue had thought of her plenty too, and not always in a platonic way.

They all lay awake in separate houses, listening to the sounds of the night and trying to starve their fears that she wouldn't come. The daybreak would come far too quickly and the clocks seemed to be ticking away every little last chance far too fast, into the darkness of what could end up being called The Night Before.

## Chapter 2

The light that streamed through the crack in the curtains made Amelia stir slightly, just enough to drift into the plane between awake and asleep, and to realize that her headache was no better. She could hear her pulse and needed water, her mouth was dry and she surprised herself with an audible groan as she sat up. She had never felt the resonance of a human voice from within a body before, it was odd.

Things felt strange, and they looked strange and sounded strange. Her squinting eyes surveyed the scene slowly, and blinked wide open along with a gasp when they caught the paper bag full of tablets. There was some wine left in one of the bottles and the sight of it made her lurch forwards as she felt the vomit start to rise in her throat. She dashed along the landing with one hand over her mouth and her dark hair flying out behind her, wretched, and wretched again.

What the hell was going on?

It took a few moments to get to her feet and flush, as she watched the swirling water take away almost two bottles of cheap plonk she felt shaky and cold. She sat on edge of the bath for a moment and took some deep breaths. Once the feeling had subsided she stood up, turned on the shower and undressed.

It ran hot, goose bumps made her shiver momentarily as the glass screen started to fog. As she tilted back her head the sensation of relief poured over her body. This was the weirdest hangover she could ever remember, all of her senses seemed amplified somehow. The sound of the water was louder than usual and now the heat was beginning to feel like tiny needles in her scalp. The smell of the shampoo was overpowering and made her feel nauseous again, as well as making the skin on her hands itch.

The towel felt slightly damp and too rough, and the feeling of her wet hair on her back made her body shudder. All she wanted to do was curl up in bed and wait for this to pass, but in reality her attendance had been borderline this year to say the least, and she needed to graduate.

She pulled on some underwear and started muddling through her chest of drawers for something half suitable. Nothing felt or looked right and ten minutes later the room resembled a yard sale. She looked at the piles of clothes and tears started to flow. Why didn't any of this make sense? She sat with her head in her hands and sobbed. A feeling of loneliness lapped at her feet and threatened to pull her under, and her head kept on aching. She crawled back under the duvet and pulled it over her head, just one more day.

Then she heard him bellowing up the stairs, "I'm going in ten minutes if you want a ride, you had better get your sorry ass into school. I don't want that Little Miss Bullshit threatening me no more!"

With her heart sinking and her head pounding Millie pulled on some jeans and the nearest sweater. She gagged once more when brushing her teeth, and by the time he had started the truck she was fastening up her coat and stuffing a banana and a can of Coke in her bag.

The ride to school was the bumpiest and most unbearable twelve and a half minutes of her life. Her stomach lurched when he lit up a cigarette. The thick, choking smell of smoke curled up her nostrils and even when he opened the window a crack, none left through the gap. The radio blared and the heater was broken. She couldn't wait to gulp in the fresh air when he pulled into the car park.

Millie muttered a thank you and stumbled out of the truck, walking quickly with her head down to the science block. She opened the door of 3a as quietly as possible, and on tiptoed feet slid into the classroom and crept to the back row next to Plain Jane Harris.

"Nice of you to join us, Millie!" said Mr. Barlow in a loud and sarcastic voice, causing her face to color up crimson.

Jane elbowed her in the ribs as soon as his back was turned and whispered "Where have you been? You know it's an assessment!"

Millie shrugged and hung her head.

"I've told you, just ignore them. Keep your head down, we're nearly out of here." She squeezed her friend's hand under the desk.

Dweebs unite.

Neither of them had ever been popular or accepted, but both of them would have gladly swapped this for just being left alone. It was like a universal irony, a cosmic double whammy. Have a crap life and then have it highlighted to everyone and get even more crap.

"You should have reported them yesterday, they went far too far," Jane said.

Tears filled her eyes as Millie's memory flashed back, there was no physical pain this time but the whole experience had shattered her. It felt like she was watching the scene from above as it all played out again like a movie. The feeling of being surrounded and unable to escape was the worst, there were six of them and they had her cornered. They'd taken her schoolbag and one of the boys had urinated in it, while one of the girls went through her coat pockets and found her cell phone. She'd videoed her being pushed up against a wire fence and held by her throat as some of them spat on her and called her vile names, while the others laughed. She'd uploaded the clip straight to YouTube on a private link so that they could all watch it over and over. They had then smashed up Millie's phone and shoved it back in the sodden bag before throwing it in her face.

Jane had found her cowering and crying in the same place, behind the sports hall, half an hour later.

"Millie! Millie, oh my god what's happened to you?" She had cradled her friend and gently rocked her as heaving sobs poured from her heart and throat. Jane cried too, not just for her friend, but because she knew. This could have easily been her, if she'd been a few minutes later getting out of gym.

"We have to report them this time, we can't go on like this." But no sooner had Jane said the words than she felt her friend's body tense up and her panicked tone rang out.

"No Jane! No! Promise me, promise me you won't say anything!" Millie's eyes pleaded with her frantically.

"Ok, ok I promise," said Jane. "But your dad is going to be furious."

"What do you mean?" sniffed Millie.

"He was waiting for you in that awful truck up on the drive for half an hour. He kept calling you and leaving messages and then eventually he drove off in a temper shouting something about the last time and you walking from now on."

"My phone..." Millie started to cry again. "They took it and they smashed it up. I was hurrying to get to the driveway when they cornered me, I was on the way and they trapped me..."

She felt Jane's arms around her again and her voice was gentle, "Oh Millie, poor, poor Millie."

Jane walked most of the way home with her, and she was grateful. The lights were on and the television was loud, the silhouette of her father with a can of beer in his hand sat on the sofa.

Millie's key turned in the lock and he muted the television.

"So you decided to come back then?" he slurred.

"I'm sorry, Dad, I tried to...," she started to answer him in a mumbled tone with her head bowed and wishing for the millionth time that he'd been the one to die and that her mother was still here.

"Tried?" He mocked her "Tried you say?" he took another swig of the can in his hand. "Tried to make a joke out of me, by leaving me bloody waiting while I'm ringing and ringing you! On the phone by the way that I bloody pay for!"

"I tried to…" she started to speak again and he cut in.

"Just get out of my sight. I don't want to see you again tonight, I've had it. As if it's not hard enough raising you on my own without all of this crap." Then he turned his back and turned up the volume as the tears streamed down her face and she made for the stairs.

She knew why he was angry and bitter, she had watched the slow erosion of the man and the father that he used to be over the past years. She had lost count of the number of times she'd cleaned him up and covered him with a blanket to sleep it off on the sofa. Millie had begged him to go for help, but he was proud and couldn't expose himself to judgment from others. It took all of his strength to keep functioning and hold down his job, and when home time came he was always desperate for a drink to numb the pain and shut off the memories that haunted him in both waking and sleeping hours. She still heard him shout out her mother's name in his sleep sometimes and cry, and this made her cry too. Then he would get up for another drink, and another.

She'd closed the bedroom door behind her and sat in relative silence, and then made her way to the bathroom, gathering up all of the medication she could find. She sat and popped each pill out of the foil strips and waited until she thought he'd be asleep then made her way past the sofa, and took two bottles of wine from the rack. They were dusty, he was a beer and spirits man. The first few gulps made her cough, but once she had downed half a bottle it got easier.

It was calm in the eye of the storm, and once she felt numb and oblivious she would take the pills. Then she could leave this shitcart of a life once and for all and join her mother, and even if heaven didn't exist, she knew hell did and she wanted out.

"Amelia!" shouted the teacher loudly and it made her jump back to reality in a snap. "Are you with us today?"

"Yes sir, sorry sir," she mumbled and turned to the right page in her textbook, feeling all twenty-two pairs of eyes burning holes in her, humiliation burning up her complexion once again.

"Please let this day pass quickly," she thought, "I feel so *Alien*."

## Chapter 3

Orin suddenly froze.

"What is it?" asked Blue.

"I think I hear her...," Orin answered. "It's faint, but I think that she could be close... do you see anything?"

Blue closed his eyes, and they flickered beneath his eyelids for a moment.

"I see that things are changing, we have a chance now, I don't see her, but I see that there are now two paths for the outcome instead of one... she must be here."

For a second they forgot where they were, and a spontaneous high five was met with a look of disdain from the librarian. They lowered their voices.

"We need to track her, lock in on her thoughts and energy field and find her as fast as we can," said Orin. The librarian was making her way to their desk now and they stood up ready to leave before she had the chance to evict them.

"Make sure you are open, keep checking and anything at all that you can get, let me know. Just think loud and I will hear you. I'll move between you and her until I get something..." Orin started walking along the long corridor that led to the sports hall and Blue took the door that led outside to the grounds. They moved quickly and quietly, with an awareness of each other, and everyone else in the vicinity.

Upstairs in the science lab Millie fumbled with the safety goggles and the teacher once again went over the experiment. He announced that they now had half an hour to conduct all of the steps on the white board, write up the findings, evaluate and hand in.

Jane lit the Bunsen burner and the flame flickered orange and blue, they measured colored liquids into test tubes and stirred with a glass rod. There were murmured voices, the clink of glass on glass, and the tick of the teacher's pen as he prowled around workstations and observed each pair in turn.

Millie carefully lifted one of the test tubes from the rack with the scissor type clamps and held it in the flame.

*Where are you?* Orin's voice filled her head with an echo that sounded familiar, yet not.

"I'm here," she answered out loud, and the teacher's pen stopped ticking.

Orin stopped dead in his tracks, with his first foot on the bottom step of the flight of stairs that led to the science block. He focused his energy again. "Where are you?" he thought and projected it as far as he could around the building. She had heard him, and that could only mean one thing, that she was a telepath too.

Everyone in the room turned to stare at Millie, she could feel their gaze and her face burning red with embarrassment. She busied herself with the experiment and wished the ground would open up and swallow her.

Then she heard him calling again, and this time realized that no one in the room had uttered a sound.

She looked around wide-eyed and afraid, and the test tube started to break in the heat with a loud crack. Bright blue liquid bubbled over onto the desk top test paper. Millie dropped the tongs and shrieked as it splattered up her bare arms and the glass shattered on the floor.

"Get out! Get out of my head!" she pulled off the safety goggles and looked around her at the sniggering faces and Jane's wild stare.

"Millie, calm down!" she said through gritted teeth and started to dab paper towels on her bare and scalded forearms. Millie felt tears brimming over her lower lids and her head pounded loudly.

Orin had heard the shriek and like a radio tuned to the right frequency he could hear Millie FM loud and clear. Her energy was definitely not one that he had felt in school before, but he had heard her voice. Familiar in some ways yet totally different in others, like a whole new person was in the same body... and that meant only one thing – A Walk In.

Orin knew firsthand how confusing this process was, he was fully integrated now and awake to the soul that lived inside of him, but this had taken years. They didn't have that much time.

*What's happening to me? I'm a freak, I just want to get out of here. I hate it here... please help me someone...*

He followed her thoughts and scaled the steps two at a time.

The moment that Millie fled from the classroom he was ready to catch her. The girl that had been invisible to him for years and completely irrelevant now held the fate of humanity in the palm of her hand, and she had absolutely no idea.

## Chapter 4

Orin ushered her down the stairs and into a cupboard that reeked of disinfectant. The long handles of brushes and mops clattered together as he pulled the door closed and spoke to her in a hushed tone. Millie only heard the odd word here and there, she was sobbing and shaking and although Orin's soothing voice calmed her a little, she still felt panic and confusion grip her tightly.

"Who are you?" she stammered. "What's going on? I've woken up in some kind of freak show and nothing makes sense..."

*Breathe.*

"I am breathing for God's sake, it's just fast..."

*Breathe slowly.*

She took a deeper breath, and then another and felt her heart rate slow a little. She even managed to look at him now her eyes had adjusted to the dim light in the janitor's store, and she realized that he was beautiful. In fact this was the closest that she had been to someone of the opposite sex, never mind someone who looked like this. And he was touching her, his arms gently held her by the elbows and he looked at her with intense eyes and a paradoxical mixture of concern and elation written all over his face.

*That's it, breathe slowly.*

"Ok, ok, now will you tell me what is going on here? And why we are hiding in here?" *He's yummy, I don't really care why I am here I am just glad that I am.* "And what are you doing with my mind? You're talking to me without talking? It's freaking me out!"

A smile broke across Orin's face and he suppressed a chuckle. "I should tell you right away that this *really* will freak you out but, erm, it's the decent thing to do so...," he released his grip on her arms and ran his fingers through his hair.

"Tell me what?" Millie hissed. *Tell me anything you like, I like you....*

"Well you won't believe me but I can hear your thoughts." He half smiled and waited for her reaction.

*Like Hell You Can.*

"Like hell I can," he said out loud and her expression changed to one of intrigue and shock.

*You are shitting me.*

"I am not shitting you," he replied, and shrugged. "It's part of what I can do."

*No Way.*

"Yes Way."

"Would you stop that already?" she hissed again. *What the hell is happening to me? Trapped in this weird sci-fi scenario with a hunk of a guy in a cupboard?*

"Thanks," he said. "I can explain you if you want me to, but you have to have an open mind."

"Stop it!" she made to push past him and he gripped her arm again.

"Amelia, please…"

*It's Millie.*

"OK. Millie, please let me and the others explain." His eyes pleaded with her, and his tone sounded serious now.

"There are others?" she asked. "How many of you are there?"

"You are the fourth," he said.

*Now I know you are crazy.*

"I'm being honest, really I am Millie, please give us a chance and we will explain everything." He looked into her eyes intently, and something stirred within her.

*Either you are telling the truth or are completely delusional.*

"I'm not delusional, please give us a chance," he said.

*I've got nothing to lose.*

He smiled at her. "You're right, you have nothing to lose."

21

And with that he slowly opened the door and led as they made their way towards the fire exit.

## Chapter 5

Once they were out in the open air, another figure ran towards them. Millie recognized him, but he looked at her inquisitively, then turned to Orin raising one eyebrow.

"Yes," said Orin, and then, "No," and then, "I know," and the conversation that she could only hear half of flashed in their eyes as Orin apparently read the other's thoughts.

*What's his name again,* she thought?

"Oh sorry, this is Blue." Orin turned to her.

"Stop doing that!" Millie said.

"Sorry," replied Orin, "it's what I do."

"Well don't!" She spat the words at him and folded her arms across her chest. "This is weird enough for me as it is."

The guys looked at each other and Blue shrugged.

Orin softened his expression and turned to face her.

"Look Millie, I'm sorry. I know that this must be freaking you out."

*You don't say.*

"I know that things feel totally weird and all over the place for you at the minute, and that we're overloading you…"

*With crap.*

Orin sighed.

"Please Millie, just trust me for a moment, it's all I ask and we'll show you what we mean."

Millie shook her head.

*Why should I trust you, you've never even said hello to me before today?*

"I know our paths have never crossed before, but they have now… isn't there even the smallest part of you that is at least curious?"

The bell sounded loudly and kids stared to pour out of the building like scurrying ants, covering the walkway and heading for the canteen or the street. Among the crowd Millie saw a girl heading their way, impish and petite with big green eyes and freckles.

"Hey," she said as she joined them, and looked Millie up and down then turned to the guys expecting an explanation.

"Yes we are sure, Emma," said Orin out loud and she looked embarrassed.

"OK, just wondering! She doesn't look the way I thought she would, that's all." Emma forced a smile in Millie's direction and Millie gathered what her loaded statement had meant, but to add more substance to it Emma's thoughts rang out in her head as well.

*Jesus Christ. Look what the cat dragged in.*

"No need to be so catty yourself!" Millie snarled, and Orin stepped between them.

"Emma!" His tone was stern now. "Yes it's her, and she is a telepath like me, it's just intermittent at the moment because it's new."

*Shit.*

"Shit indeed!" Millie retorted and Emma blushed. "And for the record, I didn't ask to be tele-whatsit, I'd far rather step out of this freak show and get on with graduating if it's all the same to you guys." Millie could feel her face flushing and her tears threatened to spill as she continued. "Look, I know that you saved me from a nightmare chemistry lesson and all, but this isn't for me... I mean you can get on with your gang of weirdo friends and all and your Start Trek party tricks, but if you don't mind David Blaine, I'm just going to get back to the life that I had. Granted it was monumentally shit but at least it wasn't shit *and* weird..." She made to walk away from Orin after she'd finished speaking, but her thoughts continued to ring out as she saw her tormentors from yesterday striding towards her.

*Oh no, no, no...*

And then the strangest thing happened. To Millie it was as if time stood perfectly still all around her and she was able to move, influence, and make changes to the scene while everyone else saw things in real time. From her vantage point she found that she could anticipate what was going to happen next, get a feeling for it somehow and even see still shots from the imminent future. She saw herself being pushed hard against a wall by one of them and then tripped up by another, badly grazing her knee and the palm of her hand, crying and cowering as Orin and Blue rushed to pick her up, then *Rewind.*

None of this had happened yet, and as she thought about the possibility of a different scenario, the pictures started to morph and change into the new reality that she could seemingly mold and adapt to her vision. *You are losing the plot, Millie Spielberg.* In her mind's eye Millie added one finishing touch to the picture in her head. *Wishful thinking.*

She braced herself for the shove that she'd seen coming and closed her eyes. Laughter broke out spontaneously around her and as she dared to look, she even dared to join in when she saw the ringleader lying on the path with a bloodied nose that had collided with the curb when his trousers fell round his ankles and tripped him up. The scene played out just as she had visualized.

He didn't know where to cover up, his nose as it squirted out blood and bright red snot, or his manhood, which to be fair was hardly bigger than his nose really. He could have used a hand for each.

*Serves you right, you bastard.*

Orin turned and looked at her.

*You did that,* he projected loud and clear.

She looked at him as panic and victory combined in her expression.

"I did?" she asked him quietly.

*I think so, Millie, I think you did.* He smiled at her, and although she tried to fight it in this crazy moment, the corners of her mouth smiled slightly too.

## Chapter 6

"Will you come with us and let us explain?" asked Orin.

His eyes were beautiful, rich and brown, and framed with the longest thick black lashes that any girl would wish to have been blessed with. His hair was dark as well with a natural flick at the front, a cow lick that no doubt his mother spent hours trying to tame when he was a child.

"Millie?" he asked again and she sighed.

"I'm just worried that something might happen to me if I go somewhere with a group of people I don't really know." She hung her head.

*They really hurt me, I wanted to die.*

She sniffed back tears and for the second time today felt Orin's strong arms around her. Emma rolled her eyes impatiently and Orin shot her a cold stare as he read her thought - *Drama Queen.*

They stood for a moment longer and Millie could hear Emma and Blue shuffling impatiently, but she wanted to prolong the feeling of being safe, she couldn't remember the last time she'd had that.

Orin sensed that she was ready for him to release the embrace and his arms gently fell to his side.

*I promise I will take care of you, Millie.* He projected into her mind and took hold of her hand, staring at her intensely. It felt like his eyes were reflecting the whole intention of the universe at that moment and she felt herself surrender.

*I believe you.*

And a memory of being held and loved flashed through her mind, in a faraway time and place that she couldn't hold on to for more than a few seconds. It was vivid enough in that moment of recall to immerse herself in the emotion completely, she closed her eyes to connect more fully, but it drifted.

*Home.*

Emma impatiently clearing her throat brought Millie back to reality with a jolt.

"Look I'm sorry for sounding impatient guys but what's happening here?" she asked.

Orin looked at Millie and she took in a deep breath.

"Ok, I'll come with you," she said. "But where exactly?"

The three exchanged glances as if Millie wasn't there and Orin spoke first.

"We start with the book?" he said and the other two nodded.

Emma placed her hand over the front of the large brown leather satchel that she had slung across her shoulder. It fastened with two silver buckles and the leather was worn. "I'm on it," she said.

"Ok, now where?" Orin turned to Blue as he closed his eyes for a moment and spoke about the wooded area at the back of the school that was surrounded by wire fencing. "It's clear for the next hour," he said and they all turned to start walking in that direction.

*I don't get it.*

"You will get it, don't worry," smiled Orin and took her hand.

They made their way along a dirt track, the gate wasn't locked, but it had been, the thick heavy chain was cut and lay in the nettles near the gatepost, along with the padlock.

Blue pulled the gate open enough to squeeze through, there had been heavy rain and mud had washed up around the bottom. The gate scraped it back into a little pile leaving a combed pattern in the wet ground.

"Ladies first," he gestured to Emma and Millie and as Millie passed him so closely the ice blue color of his eyes shone bright and clear.

*That's why they call him Blue.*

"Yeah," said Orin, who was one step behind and obviously well within range to stay locked into her thoughts.

28

They walked along the dirt track a little further until they came to a clearing with a couple of tree stumps that could act as chairs. Orin gestured to Millie to take a seat and Emma started to unfasten the satchel. She needed both hands to pull out the heavy, old leatherbound book in blood red with a golden infinity symbol etched onto the cover..

"The Book of Time," she said and placed it with a not too gentle thud in Millie's lap.

Millie ran her finger over the symbol and looked up at them watching her.

*So it's just some old book.*

Orin laughed. "Millie it's not just some old book, that's your ego butting in. Do you think that we would have brought you down here just to look at some old book?"

Millie shrugged. "I don't know, in fact there's a load of stuff happening that I don't know about right now, I don't think anything could surprise me!"

The two guys looked at Emma and they all laughed at the irony of what was coming next.

"Oh you're going to be surprised alright!" said Emma and the others agreed. "Go on, open it."

Millie opened the cover and saw that the pages were old and yellowed. The writing was in a scrolling font that was beautiful but difficult to read, and the teachings were poetic and cryptic as she scanned the first few lines. The first paragraph spoke of the creation of the Earth and sounded in parts quite biblical. There were references also to energy and matter, light and darkness, good and evil. As she read each word there was a feeling of deep resonance within her as if she were being told a story that had been passed down through many generations, it rang true in her heart and she felt emotional and a strange feeling, rather like homesickness.

Millie raised her head and looked at the three others. "What's happening?" she asked them in a quiet voice like a lost child.

"You are reading the story of Time," Emma replied. "Of All That Is."

Silence fell for a moment as Millie's conscious mind struggled with this.

"We've all read it," said Blue, "it's a total mind flip and it will take you a while to believe, never mind understand."

"It's coded," said Orin and Millie looked perplexed. "I mean it's got energetic codes running through it, and when you read it you will download these codes into your energy body and they will be activated so that you embody what you need to."

Millie shook her head in disbelief.

"So it's *alive*?" she said.

"You could say that," said Emma, "and you certainly will be when you have finished it."

Millie looked down at the thickness of the book and the tiny ornate calligraphy letters and doubted that she'd be finishing this anytime soon.

"Don't worry about reading it word for word, you will *absorb* some of it, a lot of it in fact just by using your intention and turning the pages," said Orin.

Millie wanted to laugh out loud at the absurdity of such an idea, but something in his stare and her gut feeling told her that this was possible, in fact it felt like a subtle vibration was emanating from the book and into her body as she sat there with it resting on her knees.

"Ok, I can buy that," she said, "but what exactly do I have to read this for anyway?"

"To find out who you are." Emma's tone empathized now with Millie, she knew that this part was hard and that it would shake up her life beyond recognition. Emma could still recall feeling weird and not fitting in, wanting to be liked and then finding out that she could do all of these strange things and not being believed by others. Just wanting to be normal, and being so lonely in a bubble of self-loathing for so long, before she found the others.

"You'll find it strange at first and part of you will resist the truth, but in your heart you'll know," she said as Millie's eyes widened.

"Know what?" she asked and started to sound scared.

*It's ok*, projected Orin.

"Know that you are different," Emma continued.

*Slow down.....*

"Ok," she said to Orin and then, "sorry, I know it's all a bit fast," to Millie.

"Blue, you explain it," she said and stepped back a little.

Blue cleared his throat, paused for a moment and when he spoke, his words were considered.

"You are a lightworker like us, Millie, we are different from other people. We've got abilities that they haven't and it's because we are here to make changes and help humanity." He paused to see how she would react. She continued to look at him in anticipation.

"We can all do different things, Orin is a telepath and from what I can gather so far so are you. I am a seer so I can see future possibilities and make predictions about what is going to come to pass. Emma has telekinesis and she can move things at will." He smiled at her, "I know it sounds crazy."

"I think I am hallucinating," said Millie. "I think you just said that you all have some kind of superpowers?" She snorted out a laugh and the others looked at one another and joined in. The irony was about to be unleashed when Millie realized that she was also laughing at herself.

The others stopped first and Millie's voice rang out for a few seconds longer, until she saw that they were all looking serious again.

"So I'm a telepath?" she said, her voice hinting at sarcasm.

*YES YOU ARE.*

The others laughed and Millie jumped a little.

"You did that?" she asked Orin, who was learning how to project to groups of people at the same time.

*YES I DID.*

"But, I can hear you and you're not talking!" Millie shook her head and covered her ears. "It's got to be some kind of trick, right?"

*No tricks Millie, it's all real.*

"Me next?" Emma asked and the guys nodded.

Millie watched with her mouth agape as Emma locked her vision and intention onto a stick lying at her feet and it started to move up to her waist height. Emma reached out her hand and opened her palm and caught it neatly.

"No way!" Millie shrieked. "I don't believe you just did that!"

Emma laughed and turned her attention to an old crumpled soda can. It soon began to hover over to her. As it began to drop from head height she swung the stick like a baseball bat and hit it squarely into a nearby pine tree. "Home run!" she yelled as the can wedged in the crook between the wide trunk and one of the lower branches.

"Oh my God!" Millie sounded astounded, they all laughed and remembered the excitement and awe that they had experienced when they first accepted that this was all a reality.

"Over to you, Mr. Blue!" Emma threw him the stick and although he had his back to her, in a flash his left arm swung out wide and caught it without a visual.

"Saw it coming five minutes ago," he said coolly, and turned to smile at her. She blushed a little and tucked her hair behind her ear.

"You guys are amazing!" said Millie. "I can't believe this stuff! It's awesome, you are like superheroes! Don't tell me, you're all invincible as well right?"

"Not exactly, we have human bodies and all of the normal stuff that goes with that," Emma said and cheekily untwisted a pine cone from above to drop on Blue's head. He stepped to the side a fraction before it hit him and laughed at her.

"And you say that I can do things too, like you Orin?"

"From what I have seen and heard so far you are a telepath like me, but after seeing what you did to Jason Quinn a moment ago I think that there's more to your abilities than just that."

"What do you mean, what I did?" Millie asked and the others listened closely.

It had been prophesied in the book that she held on her lap, when the fourth person was connected with the other three that there would be an acceleration in their own abilities, but also that she would come with something extraordinary. They had all been waiting to find out what it was.

"I don't understand it completely yet but I think that you can travel through the Matrix and make changes to events, people and things. I've only heard of this once before and I think it's called Shifting. It's like being able to change details in something as it unfolds to create a different outcome, like directing a movie in your mind's eye a split second before real time and then watching it happen," said Orin.

He looked at Blue with his head slightly cocked to one side as if questioning his understanding also.

Blue's lips pressed together as he closed his eyes for a second and took a breath.

"Ah yes, a Shifter." He smiled at Millie. "Good to have you on board."

The three of them exchanged glances of what looked like relief and excitement.

"But you have to practice," Blue continued. "In the now time, and then work up to the future and the past."

Orin shook his head and laughed.

"I knew it!" he said. "Blue, how far can you see?"

Blue's eye's glazed over for a moment and he seemed to be looking far away into the distance, then as he shot a look directly at Millie and spoke. "Only about three, maybe four weeks for now but it looks like you are mastering Shifting quite impressively Millie."

"What do you mean the Matrix?" Millie asked.

"The Matrix is the fabric that holds reality together, it's the time-space continuum that is connecting everyone and everything all of the time. You see in reality there is no such thing as time as we know it from a human perspective, in energy terms everything is happening all at once," Blue said.

"That's crazy," answered Millie.

"Yes it sounds crazy, but you will get your head around it Millie, especially if you are a Shifter. You'll need to start to practice making changes and influencing outcomes, but you will also have to make sure that these changes do not have a detrimental domino effect," Orin said and Blue nodded in agreement.

"Domino effect? What do you mean?" Millie looked in disbelief at all she was being told and Orin shot Blue a sideways glance.

*Too much too soon?*

Blue subtly shook his head.

*We need her up to speed fast.*

Emma walked over to where Millie was sitting and crouched down beside her, she put her hand on her knee before she spoke. "It's a lot to take in, we know, we've all been through this and to start with it's so scary. But we are with you and we'll help you."

Millie's voice cracked with emotion as she answered whilst looking down at her feet, "But I don't get it, why me? What if you are tricking me? Maybe you're making fun of me just like all the others." Emma sighed and put her arms around Millie.

"Look I am sorry for having an attitude when we met a moment ago, but I have been the only girl in this gang for a while now and sometimes I get a bit of diva fever because of that... but once you get to know me you will understand that I just need shouting down once in a while."

Millie hugged her back and fought the tears. "This is the weirdest day I have had in my life," she said after a deep breath, and they all laughed.

"It's not going to get much better I'm afraid," said Orin and Emma stepped back. "We need to explain the rest, but we haven't got time now."

He looked at Blue who zoned out for a second and then replied, "Ten minutes."

"There's more?" Millie gasped.

"There's more alright," Emma said as she closed the book with both hands and slipped it back into her satchel.

"You've had enough for now." Orin reached for Millie's hand and she got to her feet. "We can try to meet up later tonight and tell you the rest."

Millie's first reaction was to tell them no way, that there wasn't a cat in hell's chance that she would be sneaking around at night meeting up with people she hardly knew. There was, however, a feeling growing within her that some would learn to call intuition. She *knew* that she was meant to connect with them even though her fear and anxiety were playing full out.

They walked back towards the gate and once they had all passed through Orin went to pull it closed.

"Just leave it," chuckled Blue as two men on mountain bikes came around the corner and pedaled through it.

Orin and Emma laughed and Millie couldn't help but crack a smile too, maybe this was going to be OK.

## Chapter 7

Millie lay fully-clothed in her bed, under the duvet, listening to the sounds of her father's bedtime routine and faraway echoes from Orin. She screwed her eyes up tightly and held her breath whilst she pushed the thought *Not Yet* back to him and waited for his reply.

Time seemed to have slowed down as she waited in the darkness and uncertainty fluttered in her solar plexus. Eventually she heard the familiar rhythmic snoring from the next room.

*OK.*

She thought as loud as she could and projected into Orin's energy field the way that he had told her to do, she still didn't know if any of this was getting through and if in fact any of this was really happening.

*Come downstairs.*

She jumped a little when she heard his reply and wondered if she would ever get used to this. The duvet folded back and she considered putting some pillows underneath it in case her father looked in.

*No need, he's not up until 6.*

Millie jumped again and caught her breath, she would have to watch what she was thinking about from here on in, would she ever have any privacy again?

*Don't worry, I will show you how to cloak your thoughts.*

She grimaced as she slipped her feet into her training shoes and her mind shouted back *ENOUGH ALREADY!*

She was creeping down the stairs and pulling on her jacket when she heard him again.

*Sorry.*

The handle creaked a little as she held her breath and listened, but there was no break in her father's breathing. For a second the cold air drifted into the doorway, then Millie gulped back her fear and stepped out into the night.

"Hey you," whispered Orin and appeared from behind her father's truck.

"Hi, I'm sorry for erm shouting?" Millie replied.

"No, I am the one that should be sorry Millie, I should respect that you are new to this and I need to teach you how to have better telepathic boundaries. We can talk on the way." He reached for her hand and she paused for a second.

"Are you sure this is ok? I mean, I trust you, at least I think I do but this seems really weird if you don't mind me saying."

"I know it does, and I'm sorry that we have to fast track you through all of this but the truth is we haven't got long." Orin looked serious.

"Long 'til what?" Millie questioned him with her head on one side and her breath puffing clouds into the darkness.

*You don't want to know.*

"I do want to know!" she hissed and pulled back her hand, and then regretted it when she saw a wounded look spread over Orin's face.

"I don't mean that I don't want you to know Millie, it's just that it's scary, and it's easy to forget that you are new to all of this. We don't want to overload you." His concern was genuine, she felt it in her gut as well as hearing it in his tone. She gingerly reached out to him.

"My turn to say sorry now," she said and his eyes locked onto hers and he smiled.

*Don't think about liking him!*

Then he laughed and she was glad that Orin could not see her cheeks staring to burn with embarrassment under the glow of the streetlight.

"Where are we going then?" she changed the subject.

"Somewhere really magical," he said and his smile melted her fears in a single moment. "Don't worry, we'll look after you, the others are waiting, I can hear them getting impatient, let's go."

They walked towards the woods and although Millie's mind kept drifting back to her father and the possibility of him waking up, she was totally intrigued by Orin's conversation. He started by telling her how to cloak her thoughts so that other telepaths could not read them, and then went on to group projection. He touched on stealth thoughts and how telepaths could disguise their thoughts as someone else's in order for the receiver to think that it was actually their own thought, and he mentioned that this was something that was rarely done for good and that it was something to be aware of.

"The good thing about all of this is that I can help you to practice at any time of day or night," he said. "As long as you aren't cloaked at the time."

The sound of their voices rang out into the forest as they passed through the open gate and followed the smell of smoke.

"Tell them we're coming," said Orin.

"What?" Millie sounded surprised.

"It's rude to sneak up on people and it's good practice for you. Tell them we are coming and read their thoughts coming back. I'll read them too so we know you are right." Orin stopped walking and looked at her. "Go on!"

"Ok, ok, just give me a second." Millie closed her eyes and quickly locked into the energy signature of Blue and Emma and announced, "Hey guys, we are nearly with you."

As fast as a blink two messages bounced back in to her awareness and although they merged as she received them, it was possible to hear the separate voices as Emma answered, "OK," and Blue, "Cool."

"It takes some practice when you project to a group. When the information comes back you get the whole lot, and it's sometimes like listening out for a single instrument in an overture."

"Right," said Millie, rather pleased with herself.

*And so you should be.*

Blue stood up as they approached the clearing.

"Glad you could make it," he said to Millie and Emma smiled and nodded.

"Me too, well at least I think so," answered Millie, feeling nervous.

"We should get started," said Orin and gestured for Millie to sit near the fire.

"Where to start?" asked Orin and as the three of them exchanged glances, Millie heard ideas without a word being spoken. They layered over each other and spoke about the book, the mission, the portal and more. And then in a second Orin was addressing her directly.

"Millie, there is so much to tell you and not a great deal of time here." He looked at Blue and inferred the question.

"Still good 'til 6am," he verified and Orin nodded a thank you.

"OK, so here's the story in brief...," Orin began, and Millie found herself in awe and disbelief in equal measure as he spoke about the battle between light and dark and the mission that they had all come to Earth to help complete.

"It's a lot to take in but it's all in the book," he said as Emma passed over the satchel and smiled.

"Good to have you on board," she said to Millie.

Then there was a brief period of silence, apart from Millie taking in a deep breath and sighing it out as her shoulders visibly relaxed.

"Well?" asked Orin.

"I feel like I have woken up in a sci-fi series on cable TV," said Millie. "I'm sorry but I may as well be honest since I am not good at cloaking my thoughts yet."

"It's fine, we expect you to feel like that. We've had longer to get used to all of this and we have been waiting for you." Orin stood up and looked at Emma.

"We have something else to show you," he said as he gestured towards the forest floor not far from where they sat at what appeared to be nothing more than a pile of leaves.

Emma sprang to her feet and squealed with delight, "I've been waiting for this moment for so long!" she said and started to raise her right hand straight out in front of her.

"Wait," said Blue and they all stopped.

"What is it?" Orin sounded a little hesitant.

Blue turned to look at Millie and his expression softened. "Millie has two choices after she sees this and we need to know that they are both equal at the moment. I see two different pathways, one with us all together and one is just dark." Millie shuddered as the gravity of her choice came to rest hard on her shoulders.

"Millie, there is a lesson coming up for you now about trust and self-belief." Blue continued, "You're going to feel like you aren't good enough to be doing this and it could sabotage you and make you bolt."

A wave of emotion started ebbing into Millie's awareness and threatened to cascade over her completely. Her own insecurities surfaced quickly and in her mind's eye she was suddenly back on her hands and knees scrambling to piece together her shattered cell phone and confidence, both equally pointless. This was the truth of who she was, a nobody and a no-hoper and no matter how Orin and Emma's pleas rang out in her consciousness, they were eclipsed by the core

41

belief that she was not worthy of anything good, and that she would never have any true friends. For all she knew this could be one big trick to get her alone so they could humiliate and bully her, just like the others did.

Orin came close to her now and cupped her face in his hands. He spoke gently. "Listen, it's ok. We're not like them and we aren't going to hurt you."

Millie refused to make eye contact and as her tears spilled over his fingers she blurted out in anger and indignation, "Why me, then? Why now? You guys couldn't be bothered to look at me before yesterday!"

Orin put his arms around her and she sobbed into his shoulder as the others watched her outburst. "It's ok," he said as he stroked her hair, he held her safe as her heart felt like it was breaking and an unidentifiable mixture of feelings flooded through her being.

"I don't know why I feel so, so, so..." she struggled to explain and he hugged her tighter.

"I know," he said over again, "I know."

"You don't know about me, you can't know what I am going through," she sobbed and Orin gently stepped back and held her at arm's length.

"I do know Millie," he said firmly now and she looked at him straight.

"What do you mean?"

"I mean that I understand that crazy mix-up of feelings that you are having and the confusion like you are living two separate lives," he said.

"You're just saying what you hear me think, it doesn't mean that you know..." Millie sniffed and started to wonder if she would be able to find her way back through the forest to her bed.

"Listen to me Millie, I know." He tilted her chin so that she had to look at him and see the sincerity in his face. "I've been there," he said and Millie felt a strange stirring within her, familiarity perhaps? In that moment she could tell that he was genuine, and also her lifeline to finding out what the hell was going on with her.

"Sit down," Orin said softly and Emma handed her a tissue.

They knew that this would be a shock and that Orin was the best one to tell her.

Orin took her hand and started to tell her his story. Millie listened intently and every now and then nodded in understanding as she compared his experience to her own.

"A Walk In or soul exchange often happens at a point of trauma or extreme challenge in someone's life, they are common after car accidents or surgery. People have reported feeling like a totally different person, and in fact they are."

"So you are literally another soul in the same body," said Emma.

Millie heard the words as her mind was taking her back to something that felt like a memory, but it was difficult to lock down in her consciousness. She could remember sitting huddled up in her bedroom and crying, wishing and wanting her life as she knew it to end, and then a vague recollection of connecting with someone else. But then the someone else felt like her, and the version of her that was sitting huddled up felt like it wasn't her now. This was really confusing.

"It's integration Millie," Orin said as he read her thoughts. "You have very newly Walked-In and you are integrating your high vibrational soul signature with a denser physical Earth body, and it's a process that can take a while. You will feel bipolar for a few weeks yet until you have fully anchored here and brought together all of the different frequencies that make up you. You will have access to the former soul's memories to help you to navigate around your human life, but sometimes there are gaps in these circuits. Don't be alarmed if you forget names and places, you are not going crazy!"

"Crazy would be an understatement right now," she answered, shaking her head.

"I know it's a mind flip, and along with everything else it must feel like you have been beamed onto a movie set or something." Orin tried to lighten the atmosphere, he knew that they had to get her on board.

*Come on Millie, we need you.*

She smiled weakly and turned to look at Emma and Blue. "And you? Are you guys like us too?" she asked.

"No, we awakened to who we are rather than Walking In," said Emma. "It was a slower process and probably not nearly so much of a shock."

Millie felt all eyes on her and she knew that this would be the moment to make the decision. In or out?

Could things get any weirder? Here she was sitting in the woods late at night with three people she didn't know that were telling her she had superpowers and that she was an alien.

She closed her eyes and took a deep breath, let it out slowly and then looked at the three expectant faces.

"Ok, I'm in," she said as Emma squealed with delight and nearly knocked her over backwards with an enthusiastic hug. Blue and Orin high-fived and relief was evident all round. Whatever she was getting into couldn't be worse than what she had been living through.

"Ok now?" Orin asked Blue, and Blue nodded.

They gestured to Millie to move the few steps into a clearing that she had been unaware of until now, and looked at one another. Excitement and anticipation began to rise and Emma suppressed a nervous laugh.

"This is it!" said Orin and Millie could sense him smiling in the darkness.

"What's going on?" asked Millie.

"You'll see," said Orin. "It's going to be fine, don't worry."

The next sound that Millie heard was the soft rustling of leaves as Emma stood with her arm outstretched and her palm pointing towards the Earth. The leaves swirled into a column and she effortlessly moved them to form a neat pile behind her. They revealed a stone circle that had deep carvings showing the different directions of a compass, with a five pointed star in the center. It looked ancient and more than a little creepy in the glow from the campfire over Millie's shoulder.

"You are North," Emma said to her as she shuffled to Millie's left and her feet aligned with a capital letter E. Orin took his position opposite Millie and Blue to her right. They all stood on the forest floor and glances shot to one another as Millie heard a mixture of their thoughts layering over her own, excitement, anticipation, fear and uncertainty.

*What is going on?*

Orin held her gaze for a second and a feeling of calm started to settle over Millie as she heard him say *This is the way that it's meant to be*, and she found herself nod in agreement.

"Are we all ready?" asked Emma with an excited quiver in her voice. Millie felt her head nod again and although she could feel anxiety starting to dance within her, there was a feeling of acceptance, almost inevitability.

"Orin, you should explain," said Blue.

"It's an activation, Millie," he said. "We don't really know what's going to happen, all we do know is that we've tried this before and it was no good without you. We needed to have all of the directions of the compass covered by the right person."

*This sounds crazy.*

Orin chuckled. "I know it sounds crazy, believe me, we all know it sounds crazy, and we don't know what's going to happen next so we can't tell you, which makes it even more crazy..."

"He's right, I can't see this part, as much as I'd love to," Blue added.

"And I am *desperate* to know what happens next!" squeaked Emma.

"So let me get this right," began Millie. "You guys have been waiting for your missing link all this time in order to bring her to the woods and stand on some spooky circle for something monumental to happen that you have no idea about?" she laughed nervously.

They shrugged and Emma laughed too.

"Guess so," said Orin. He looked nervously at Blue and Millie picked up his concern. *Is she going to bolt?*

Before Orin had a chance to answer, Millie projected back.

*Hey talk to me!*

"Sorry Millie, we're all just worried that this is too much too fast and that you might change your mind." Orin looked sheepish.

*Will you?*

Millie looked at them each in turn and before she knew it she felt like she was stepping out of her body and back three paces.

*Fast Forward.*

The edges stared to blur on her human vision and the images before her flickered and flew forward in time as she saw herself standing with her hands open wide and light filling them and overflowing into her heart. She intentionally shifted her perception left and then right, and in her mind's eye saw the same process happening for the others.

The image faded and she saw them laughing together in the nighttime forest, it felt like playing. Moving things at will, second guessing each other's thoughts, predicting what the next split second had in store and something she couldn't quite decipher, but then the word *connecting* came and Millie knew that this was a feeling that had eluded her for a long time.

A stick snapped in the fire and Millie felt her consciousness jolt back into her body, the others were staring at her and the question still hung in the air all around.

*Will you?*

"Let's do this," she said with conviction and a smile. The longing for real friends and acceptance finally seemed be a possibility, even if it was in the most bizarre circumstances.

*What did you see?* She heard Orin project as they all exchanged eye contact.

"I guess I just *Shifted* as you guys would say…," Millie said. "I moved into the future and I saw us."

"Saw us what?" asked Emma with excitement.

"I saw us receiving what looked like light, and then laughing and playing with our new, erm, powers…"

"Oooo what did I get?" Emma squeaked.

"They aren't new Emma, they are what we've already got but magnified," said Orin. "At least I think that's what the book meant."

"Yes, that's right," said Blue tentatively, as if he was drifting between the vision that was unfolding in his mind's eye and the current now time. "But to Millie it's all new; to us it's going to be something of an upgrade or acceleration."

"How come you can see it now and you couldn't before?" asked Emma.

47

Blue nodded in Millie's direction, "because Millie has made her mind up to be a part of this, and until then there was no certainty that this would happen."

"So what next?" Millie asked, feeling for the first time in her life like a hero.

Emma jumped in and started to explain. "We all need to stand on our compass point at the same time and ask that the activation begins. Our combined intention will activate the process. We have to hold hands at first, and then when it comes to receiving we have to make the circuit with our feet, so that we can open our hands."

"Then into our heart," said Millie and Emma smiled broadly.

"Yes, then into our heart."

"What are we waiting for?" said Orin, and his words were less of a statement and more of a question directed at Blue.

Blue shrugged. "Nothing as far as I can tell, I think it's all good to go."

And with that they all took a deep breath in and stepped forwards onto the ancient stone circle.

## Chapter 8

At first nothing happened, apart from Emma's nervous giggling. Orin looked at Blue with a questioning expression and Millie felt his energy prickle a little with anxiety. Her own heart was beating loudly in her rib cage and as Emma and Blue reached out to take her hand she worried about her sweaty palms and quickly wiped them down the front of her jeans.

The sounds of the nighttime forest seemed louder than they had been, and their combined anticipation was almost palpable.

*What now?*

Millie thought and they all turned to look at her.

*Sorry.*

She thought, for a second she'd forgotten that her thoughts were not private until she had mastered how to cloak them.

It was then that a subtle but definite vibration started to move beneath their feet, Millie tightened her grip around her companions' hands and closed her eyes.

*It's started.* She thought and the same words bounced back from each member of the circle. Their thought forms resonated around her mind as the vibration grew stronger and a rumbling began deep in the Earth.

Millie looked up and shot a glance at Orin who stood opposite her, he looked straight back into her wide and frightened eyes and she heard him tell her that it was ok, and that this was the way it was always meant to happen. She looked down at the center of the circle and could see now that there was something starting to shine through one of the sides of the star, and a cracking noise was ringing out as the stone gaped open to let brilliant white light flood through. The light followed the geometric shape one side at a time until the whole star shone like a cosmic beacon and they had to squint into its brilliance to see. The light projected the same star shape high above them into the black sky and the rumbling subsided to give way again to the subtle vibrational hum.

They all looked at each other in wonderment and Blue was the first to speak.

"The portal is open now, we need to receive and then shut it down before anyone else realizes."

Millie followed the others as they broke free from each other's grip and instead shuffled their feet outwards. She held her hands out and closed her eyes as a feeling of emotion washed over her and random images of a faraway place filled her memory. Tears ran down her cheeks as love and gratitude entered her senses, and her hands filled with warmth.

*Open your eyes.*

Millie heard Orin and as her eyelids fluttered open she caught her breath. Tiny dancing particles of every imaginable color were cascading into her hands in an iridescent rainbow. When they connected with her, they seemed to merge with the cells in her own hands, the skin now seemed paper-thin in texture and absorbent. As the energy moved down her arms, not only could she feel its warmth and tingling sensation, she could see that her hands were starting to glow. This glow pulsed in time with her heartbeat, and Millie took a second to look at the others who were all experiencing the same. The vibration through the Earth and the humming sound moved in and out of her experience, and she could feel something being pulled through her feet. She felt lighter, like she was releasing old and heavy energy, and as this left her there was another feeling that she could only liken to being gently stroked but underneath her skin.

Millie looked at her hands where she could feel the gentle touch and could see the energy weaving together, as if it was using her skin as a loom of light. One stream moved swiftly over and under the other, like strands of a living gossamer fabric. The layers of light continued to form an exact silhouette of each finger, and then floated for a split second before wrapping around each finger in turn. There was suddenly a jolting feeling throughout Millie's hands like electricity, and her skin looked perfectly normal again. The same process then started in each arm, she could feel the warmth spreading through her and then saw the glow through the seams in her jacket. The static-type shock was less of a surprise this time and she only jumped slightly as the tops of her legs began to tingle.

What's going on, she thought, as the sensation passed down through her knees and into the soles of her feet? The lace holes in her training shoes shone pinpricks of light into the dark night.

*We are being upgraded Millie*, she heard Orin project and she allowed her eyes to lift in his direction. He smiled at her and her stomach flipped, this could have been part of the upgrade but she knew that it was because she liked him, and that the heat in her cheeks had nothing to do with the waves of energy moving up and down her spine now.

Her torso was now being wrapped in a layer of warmth and the tingling sensation was traveling deep into her core. She could feel that her body was experiencing a fine tremor all over, and that the hairs on the back of her neck were beginning to stand up. The atmosphere was as charged as a heavy summer's evening just before the first clap of thunder, and instinctively Millie drew her hands up to be near her heart and allowed the light to pour in.

Nothing could have prepared her for the raw emotions that filled her and moved through her, in what seemed like a split second of eternity. She felt connected to every atom in the whole universe for that moment, and as if she could draw on every human and non-human feeling and experience all at the same time. It was like the whole sum of all universal energy in any and all shape, form and expression was within her. It was everything and it was nothing, it was past and future all compressed into one single present moment of All That Is. Her heart felt expanded, not in size but in presence and capacity for understanding and consciousness. The human condition suddenly felt explainable in all its different manifestations and guises, and Millie knew that she had been plugged in to the Matrix that she was going to be working with when she Shifted.

The intensity of the moment started to pass and she felt her heart start to compartmentalize different aspects and integrate them in energy pulses that ran up the back of her neck and into her brain. When she closed her eyes there were still images and then moving 3-D pictures of different scenes and representations, some she knew and many she didn't. At times this was fast and then sometimes slowed as if the transmission was buffering. Her head felt warm and her scalp tingled.

The images she could see were now overlaid with the weaving light energy strands, as they wrapped around her face and she breathed them in deeply. Millie could feel the same process happening in her lungs, and knew that even though she couldn't see inside her body, that each of her internal organs would now be glowing. Her brain felt like a jumble of thoughts were flying in all directions, it was confusing but there was an overriding knowing that this would pass.

Then came the final judder as if her whole body had been plugged into a socket and the switch had just been flipped, then darkness, apart from the star.

No one spoke, as they looked at one another in awe.

*Oh My God!* Millie heard Emma saying to herself over and over again as she stretched her arms out and wriggled her fingers. *Totally Insane!* she heard Blue think and Orin just stood and shook his head.

Then one by one they all started to laugh spontaneously and the mood lightened, the guys were bear-hugging and broke for a high five while Emma grabbed both of Millie's hands and squeezed them tight saying all of the Oh My God's that she'd been trying to contain.

"That was awesome!" said Orin. "Does anyone else feel totally different?"

"I feel invincible!" said Emma. "We should practice!"

"Wait!" Blue's tone cut through their mood swiftly and all eyes turned to look at him.

"What is it?" Orin asked and Millie shivered, not through cold but through fear.

"Shut it down!" Blue said "Now!"

Millie watched as the three of them all fell to their knees and in turn placed their right hand over the top of the star in the center of the circle. "Millie!" yelled Orin "You have to seal it."

"I don't know how!" Millie shouted back in a panicked tone as she became aware that the temperature was dropping rapidly.

A screeching noise pierced the night sky and there was a sound of scurrying and flapping, and as Millie felt something brush against her cheek and she opened her mouth to scream, Blue grabbed her right arm and forced her hand on top of his.

"By the power of now I seal you here, now, then and forever, so be it." Orin's voice rang out and the screeching continued for a moment, but as the light of the star beneath their palms began to fade, so did the terrifying noise. The Earth groaned as she closed the portal and it wasn't until they got to their feet that Millie realized she was crying.

"What was that?" she spluttered.

"That was The Dark Millie," said Blue, who was visibly shaken. "I don't know why I didn't see them coming in, I'm so sorry guys I've let you down."

Orin was the first to reassure him that this was not the case and Emma joined in too.

"They must have some way of getting in under your radar, it's not your fault. You know that they can change and adapt, that's what makes them so dangerous." Emma put her arms around his waist but he wouldn't make eye contact.

"I know but I am your seer, I need to be able to see what's coming and if I can't do that..."

"We haven't even tried out our upgrade yet, who knows what we're capable of now," Orin said, as they all felt Blue's self-reproach.

"Look at what Millie said, we're going to be practicing and having fun." Emma stepped back. "Right, Millie?"

"Right," Millie answered quietly, whatever The Dark was, she never wanted to be near it again.

"They must have seen the portal opening," said Orin. "Thank God we closed it down in time."

"Yeah, thank God we did." Blue sighed and then laughed a little with relief, he reached over and play punched Orin in the arm. "Let's see what you've got now then... it's ok, they've gone."

Orin punched him back. "Are you sure now? I mean you didn't exactly see them coming!" His tone was deliberately playful and Blue laughed again.

Millie sighed a deep breath out and they all turned to look her way.

"Hey, it's ok," said Emma. "In fact it's better than ok, we've been upgraded don't forget!"

"Don't you guys think we should be heading back now?" asked Millie. "I mean, we've been away ages."

"It's cool Millie, you won't need as much sleep now anyway," Orin said.

"But what if my dad finds I'm gone?" Millie's voice was shaky, and the tears threatened to start again. Before she knew it Orin's arms were around her and she buried her face deep in his jacket.

"Hey, I know you've had a shock, we all have. It's just that we are more used to this than you and we don't get spooked so easy."

*I'm scared.*

"I know you are." Orin held her face in his hands and looked into her eyes.

*I think I'm falling...*

*Integrating...*, he projected and Millie laughed.

"Come on, let's practice." Blue swept Emma up in his arms and she squirmed free, holding her arms out straight in front of her and directing a gale force blast his way. Just before it hit Blue he darted out of its way. "Saw you coming a mile away," he laughed as Emma spun round like a tornado, with forest debris flying wildly all around her.

"Try this!" Emma shouted as six sticks flew through the air in Blue's direction ready to pin him to a nearby tree trunk. They traveled so fast through the air Millie could only see a blurry streak as they whistled past. For a second she held her breath as they pierced into denim before bark, and even Emma gasped. Then Blue's laugh rang out from above and they could see him sitting on a high up branch swinging his legs with his arms folded.

"Not fair!" yelled Emma.

The laughed at her, and after a short while Blue jumped down and they made their way back to the fireside.

"So what can I do?" asked Millie.

"We don't know for sure yet, Blue?"

Blue closed his eyes for a second and then blinked himself back into the circle.

"Wow!" he said looking at Millie. "You can do some amazing stuff!"

"I can?" she replied, feeling hopeful that she was not about to mess up.

"Yes, I mean the telepath stuff will be like Orin and his upgrade is going to be useful in loads of ways, but he'll work with you and explain that, but *Shifting* will be the thing that you do best and as you master it you will find that there is little you can't influence or change." Blue's faraway expression changed to one of being impressed and he nodded and smiled. "It's going to be very good to have you on the team."

Millie wasn't used to accepting compliments and was glad that the night hid the flush in her cheeks.

"Show us!" said Emma. "Please!"

Millie stood and shrugged, "I don't really know how."

"Just have a little practice!" pleaded Emma. "Go on…"

"Wait," said Blue and they turned to look at him, "Don't push her, she's got to be ok with it first. This is far more complex than anything that we can do, there are repercussions…"

"Domino?" asked Orin and Blue nodded.

"What's that?" asked Millie.

"The domino effect, it's just a quick way of saying that one small change can start a chain reaction that can lead to a bigger event. You know like when you line them up and…"

"Boom!" Orin cut in and Blue stopped speaking in perfect time to allow his interruption.

There was silence for a split second as the gravity of this concept raced through Millie's mind, and the fear of getting things so badly wrong began to creep up on her.

*Millie, it's ok.* She heard Orin and he reached out his hand to her.

"You wouldn't have been given this if you couldn't handle it," he said as he looked into her vulnerable expression.

*What if I mess up,* she projected, as her bottom lip started to tremble a little and flashbacks came of the day outside the sports hall.

*You won't mess up!* Orin reassured her with a hug.

"This must be part of the upgrade," he said. "I can feel emotion as well as hear thoughts and also access the past situations that people have been through, as long as they are thinking of them."

A few moments passed and Orin released his hold, Millie sniffed back any remaining tears and spoke bravely.

"I could have a little practice I suppose?" She phrased the sentence as a question and waited for their response.

"Yes please!" said Emma first. "Is it ok Blue?"

"Yes, I get that it's ok but…"

"But what?" asked Millie.

"I don't know really… I know that sounds stupid, something is making me feel a bit anxious but I don't know what. I'm probably just integrating the upgrade." He smiled in Millie's direction but she felt unsure of his sincerity.

"I can do it another time," Millie said to Emma but Orin stepped in.

"No Millie, it's important that you start working with this and get your confidence up as fast as possible. If Blue says it's ok, then it's ok."

All eyes fell on her now and she took a deep breath and closed her eyes for a second, willing herself to move back into the Matrix of time and space, just like she had yesterday at school.

Millie opened her eyes and realized that there was no sound anymore, and no movement either, everything stood perfectly still around her as if there had been some kind of scheduled planetary pause. She could see the expressions on the faces of the others just as they had been, but there was no breathing, no pulse. Their energy and consciousness were still there, encapsulated in a time-space freeze-frame.

This was the weirdest feeling ever, she was with them, yet totally alone. She walked over to where Orin stood and drew close to him. She paused and looked at his beautiful features, slowly circling him and hearing her own feet kick through the leaves on the forest floor, as he stood statue-still and she stared. She tentatively reached out her hand and with her fingertips, reached up and touched his lips. There was no response in him but she could feel her heartbeat quicken at the thought of kissing him. She closed her eyes for a second and allowed desire to wash over her, she had felt this before but never thought that anyone could want her. Then she looked at him again. Not this time, she wanted to be with someone that wanted to kiss her back, she didn't want to take from him when he was unaware, unless it was to steal his heart completely.

Millie stepped back and wondered what to do for best effect. As soon as the intention was set to create a change, she could see, hear and feel different scenarios coming at her from all angles. It felt like she was in the middle of the most advanced information exchange, maybe like being in the middle of the World Wide Web, but this was www.allthingspossible.com.

*Closer*, she thought instinctively.

The information distilled and she felt that she was tuning into an area the size of the country. It was overwhelming. The information was layered, and it was possible to glimpse large chunks at once and then move in and out into detail and circumstance like a microscope. Freeze-frames of people's lives flickered before her like an old-fashioned cinema reel, and Millie found that once she focused on one of these the scene split into all of the different fragments of possibility that could occur.

*Closer.*

She thought again and the circle of influence around her reduced again into the size of the state, then *Closer* started to bring up scenes from her home town. This was what she was looking for. Millie quickly scanned through the images and stopped abruptly on one of a garden shed. Nothing to look at admittedly, but there was excitement radiating from it and she knew that this was at the bottom of her road and that Jake Harrison was inside with a friend. The image of the shed broke apart like a jigsaw and revealed six outcomes, five of which were boring to say the least. These included the boys sneaking back home to bed, staying out another half an hour, sharing some chocolate, stealing a neighbor's football and chasing a cat. The image that interested Millie was quickly zoomed in, and behind their startled faces she could see the night sky ablaze with multi-colored fireworks.

*They won't be expecting that!*

Millie focused on the picture with the intention to bring it to life. As reality started to change she could perceive glimpses of Orin and Emma's faces as they lit up and looked skyward, the colors were flooding her consciousness and imminent reality, as stars shot across the blackness and Millie could feel herself connecting now to the present again, ready for the show to start. Just before she could feel herself back in the here and now she looked again at Orin, proud of herself that she had created such an amazing surprise, but his expression was changing.

Millie could feel anxiety creeping up on her as she juddered back into herself and the scene before her unfolded. All three of the others moved fluidly as if they had never stopped, and as Jake and his friend lit the first rocket and started to run away, Blue spoke seriously.

"What did you do Millie, what did you change?" There was urgency in his tone that made her start to panic.

"It was meant to be a surprise… I just wanted to surprise you all…"

"What is it Blue?" Orin asked.

"Domino," he replied and they all looked at Millie.

*Oh God what?* She thought out loud and Orin spoke to Blue.

"Damage limitation Blue, what can we do here?"

BOOM and the sky filled with a cascade of multi-colored stars and they all jumped.

"Nothing apart from Millie shifting it all back again," said Blue. "QUICKLY!"

"Millie?" Orin shouted as another BOOM rang out and the night sky was ablaze once more.

"Any moment now our parents are going to be up looking out of their bedroom windows along with the rest of the neighborhood, and checking that we are still in bed safe and sound… we're gonna be grounded for the rest of our lives guys…"

"I thought you said that we were good for hours yet?" Millie panicked.

"That was before you started setting off fireworks!" said Blue, and with that there was a whistling noise and a shower of silver diamonds overhead.

"You've got to shift it back!" said Orin. "Now, Millie!"

Millie's bottom lip began to tremble and she could feel tears threatening to spill over her cheeks as the second firework exploded.

"Your dad's up Millie…" said Blue and Millie's heart pounded.

"Go on, you can do it." Orin grabbed her shoulders and shook her gently but firmly and looked her straight in the eye. "You have to."

"Emma's brother is looking out of the window and her dad's getting out of bed reaching for the phone…"

Bang, bang, bang rang out and the sky lit up again.

"My folks are up, Millie, go back now or we are seriously screwed here," Blue said harshly in her direction.

"Ok, ok, I'll try..." Millie's voice was shaking as she spoke and she closed her eyes tight. She could feel the tears run down her cheeks as she heard Blue's voice, "Your dad's opening your door Millie..."

*Pause.*

And then things were still, and Millie was standing in a forest crying her eyes out with three people that were frozen in time, and her heart was in her mouth.

She composed herself and took some deep breaths, then focused her intention once more on entering the Matrix. After quickly locating the frames she needed of the boys lighting the touch paper on the fourth rocket, her consciousness was momentarily distracted by a picture of her father with his hand ready to open her bedroom door. Which one should she change? Or maybe both? And then Blue's voice came back to her and she heard "Domino" loud and clear. She had to get to the root of this, the first event that became the catalyst to start all of the other events that dominoed as a result, back to the beginning.

*Rewind.*

The flame shot back into the lighter that Jake held, and both friends started to walk backwards to watch the third firework from the bushes, ready to run in case they were sprung. Millie held her intention as time moved backwards and she could feel an awareness of her father falling again into the sleep state that he'd left moments earlier. Relief flooded through her as the shed appeared in her line of vision and the six initial options layered over the image. She quickly chose the image of chasing the cat and drew it into the now time, and as she came back into the present reality she could hear distant laughter and mewing.

61

She started to relax now and the feeling of coming back started to unfold, and just as Millie started to connect more fully with her physical body she became aware of something flitting in and out of her peripheral vision. She couldn't make out what it was and each time she tried to focus on it, it moved out of range. She could see that whatever it was it was black and seemed to be observing her but also trying to disguise its presence. It felt like it was hiding from her.    A shudder of dread rippled through her for a split second, and Millie opened her eyes to see the others staring her way.

"Go on then!" said Emma. "Surprise us!"

Millie shook her head in complete disbelief. "I just did," she murmured.

"What?" said Orin.

"I shifted, if that's what you call it," Millie shrugged.

"But we missed it. Blue, what do you see?" Orin asked.

"Nothing's changed, but I feel less edgy. What did you do Millie?" He turned to her as did the others.

"It all went horribly wrong, I got a domino and I had to go back and undo everything." Millie looked at the forest floor. "I messed up."

Orin drew closer to her and laughed. "No you didn't! That's amazing, you shifted reality and then went back and undid it again? That's not messing up Millie, that's awesome."

He hugged her and a feeling of guilty pleasure flushed her cheeks as she recalled her earlier urge to kiss him, which hadn't really gone away.

"So I missed it?" Emma said in an exasperated voice. "What was it?"

"Fireworks," mumbled Millie at the forest floor and they all started to laugh.

"You didn't think about the noise?" Blue chuckled.

"No I guess I didn't, sorry, that was the problem." Millie relaxed a little and laughed at herself too. "Can you see if my dad's asleep please? All of our parents were up with the noise and someone called the cops."

"It's all good," Blue reassured her and Orin shook his head and laughed again.

Millie breathed a sigh of relief.

"Let's stick to telepathy lessons for the next day or so," she said and Orin smiled at her.

*OK*, she thought and smiled back.

"What time is it?" asked Emma, and Blue answered, "2:37am, we should get back."

"I don't even feel tired yet," Millie spoke as they made their way back towards the track that led through the woods and up to the gate.

"We'll probably all need even less sleep now we've been upgraded," Emma said. She sniggered as Blue shot his hand up into the air and caught the sizable horse chestnut that she'd launched at him a fraction of a second ago.

"Too slow," he mocked her and things felt good, like Millie was a part of something at last, even though it was the strangest something that she could have ever imagined.

They soon reached the edge of the woods and the leaves underfoot turned to pavement. They stood under the first lamppost to say goodnight. Orin walked Millie home and when he hugged her goodbye she breathed him in and did her best to cloak the thoughts that were racing through her mind just as fast as her heartbeat. It was probably her imagination that made her think that he'd held the embrace a split second longer than a friend would. As he tucked her hair behind her ear she caught his gaze and allowed herself to think for a moment that he might like her too.

"See you at school!" Orin called over his shoulder and ran off into the night, and Millie closed the front door as quietly as she could and crept up the stairs, wondering if he would be able to hear her dreaming, about him of course.

## Chapter 9

Millie's eyes snapped open and she caught her breath, her brow was coated with beads of sweat and her pulse fluttered quickly through her veins. She was being chased by someone or something that felt dark and terrifying it was gaining on her fast and felt bigger than her. She felt herself stumble and heard it moving in, ready to tower over her. Her instincts told her that this was male but it seemed to have a man's frame, long and athletic and cloaked in the accumulated fears and nightmares of humanity. Shredded hopes and dreams turned dark and desperate that flapped around its ankles and wrists as hands reached out for her and held tight to her terror. She had screamed herself awake and lay fighting for breath. She hadn't had nightmares for years, and hoped this wasn't the beginning of more.

Millie waited still in the darkness for the anxiety to pass, and became aware of the muffled, generalized stream of voices that she could hear. The odd word or voice stood out every now and then but it was like being in the middle of a crowd and hearing one symphony of noise made up from the many different people.

Millie thought and focused her intention on turning them down. The voices withdrew in groups and after a moment she could hear less of them. This continued and she had an awareness that some of the voices sounded more familiar. She could pick out Mrs. Blackett from school, her friend Jane and some others that she knew. Then came the moral dilemma, was this like spying? With that thought she closed down the circle more but not before she'd waited to hear Orin.

*Where are you,* she thought, listening.

*Hey, Millie.*

She heard back and jumped a little. She had forgotten to cloak her thought so he'd heard her loud and clear. That would teach her for trying to snoop.

*Oh, erm, hey Orin, do you wake up with voices in your head?*

*Yes, they aren't usually that loud, it must be the upgrade helping us to receive the thoughts from a bigger area. The information comes through faster now, like telepathic broadband instead of dial up I guess.*

*Right. I don't know if I'll ever get used to this*, Millie answered.

*It's early days Millie, you've just walked in, give yourself a break, you are doing fine*, Orin reassured her and she smiled a little. *You need to practice being able to search all of the voices and then laser in on the one you want, it's like tuning a radio to the right station. Otherwise you just get an overload. You must be doing ok, you found me!*

They talked until Millie heard her father wake; she was glad of the distraction and did all she could not to think about the dream. Orin didn't want some neurotic girl dumping all of her crazy stuff on him. They covered more about cloaking, projecting, working with groups and more, and with her head buzzing Millie climbed out of bed and headed for the shower. She had engaged full cloaking mode for now, she didn't think Orin would want to take a shower with her, and with that thought she felt herself blush.

The journey to school was the same as ever, and her father was his usual grumpy self. Millie sank into the seat and looked out of the window, willing time to pass more quickly so that she could escape his incessant negativity. The second time he slammed on the brakes and started shouting at the 'idiot driver in front', she had to bite her tongue and remind herself to stay calm. He was the idiot, she knew that only too well and she knew just as well that making any kind of comment would escalate into a full-blown argument in seconds.

"Just stay calm, you're nearly there," she told herself, and remembered that she was still fully cloaked. She had learned the basics from Orin that this could be altered in an instant, and as she deliberately thought *On*, the voices of many started to stream into her awareness. One was a little louder than the others, and she felt drawn to it through both familiarity and an overwhelming emotion that she had only ever truly felt once, despair.

"Jesus Christ!" her father shouted again and blasted his horn, she swallowed back tears as she heard him loud and clear now, not from within the car but from deep within his own pain.

*I don't know how much longer I can go on for, I can't cope with all of this anger and pain, I just want to end it all. I'm driving her away and she's all I've got left, I can't be a good father to her, it's for the best if she goes. I am a worthless piece of shit, just need to try and keep going, maybe there's a way out of this, oh God, please someone help me... I need a drink.*

Millie felt a lump in her throat and tears threatened to stream down her face so she kept her head turned towards the window. The behaviors that she had labeled as unreasonable and destructive would have been far more accurately viewed as desperation. Her father was drowning, but the person that he was projecting out into the world was pushing everyone away that had ever tried to save him.

The car slowed now to turn up the school driveway and her father sighed as he pulled into a parking bay.

"You want a ride home?" he asked.

*Who would want to ride with you, she probably hates you like everyone else.*

Millie cleared her throat and sniffed back her tears.

"Sure, Dad."

"Ok then, see you at four." He looked dead ahead through the windshield, as if making eye contact with her would crack the dam he had built to surround his feelings, and risk a tsunami of pain.

*Got to get through this and start living again one day.*

Millie's hand opened the door of the truck and as her feet hit the tarmac she paused, called on all of her strength and through a voice loaded with emotion she said simply, "I love you, Dad."

She saw him close his eyes and draw in a deep breath as he hung his head and tightened his grip on the steering wheel.

"I love you too, Millie."

*Don't let her see you cry for God's sake, she's been through enough! Drive you idiot.*

Millie walked away and heard the truck's engine roar and her father's cries for help in different ways but with equal intensity, as she made her way into the building.

## Chapter 10

Jane's smile changed to a look of concern as Millie took her seat in class.

"What's wrong?" she mouthed when the teacher's back was turned.

"Just my dad," Millie mouthed back and Jane nodded, she was the only person that really knew what Millie had been through.

Mrs. Wilson started to shuffle through a pile of papers and before she'd had the chance to announce it, Millie heard her think about the surprise algebra test that they were going to have to sit. A moment later, as the groans and objections rumbled around the room, Millie smiled to herself.

"Time for a little practice," she thought and the scene she was sitting in froze at her intentional command to *Pause*.

Once in the Matrix of possibilities Millie found that she could move backwards in order to read the answers as Mrs. Wilson was writing the questions last Tuesday in front of her television at about 10:07pm, or she could move forwards about half an hour from now after the marking of the test, and sneak a peek at the answers on the board.

It would be nice to get full marks for a change, but wait - *domino*. These test results were going to be used to choose students that were gifted and talented at mathematics and put them into an ability group for high-fliers, grooming them towards careers that would suit.

Maybe the middle ground would be a better option then, it meant less correct answers to remember anyway.

*I could get used to this*, Millie thought to herself and chuckled as she handed in her paper just before the bell.

"What's up with your dad then?" asked Jane as they made their way down the corridor.

Millie sighed and shook her head. "I dunno, I guess he's the same as he's always been, I just started thinking that maybe I should try to help him a bit more."

"You've tried Millie, honestly don't beat yourself up about it, just stick to plan A and graduate then you can look for a job out of town and leave." Jane squeezed her hand.

"I know, I just think that maybe I gave up on him too soon, that's all. He's a wreck without my mom and after all he went through..."

"And after all you went through, too. You've done your best Millie, if he can't get help then you can't do it for him, honestly you need to save yourself here." Jane had joined the queue for the vending machine and was looking for change when Millie caught a glimpse of Orin across the hall.

"I mean, he needs professional help Millie, you can't do that and until he gets it, you're stuck..."

*Hey.*

Millie smiled and tucked a strand of hair behind her ear, she could feel herself blush a little.

*Hey you.*

"Millie! Are you listening to a word I'm saying here?" Jane nudged her and the clunk of the soda can being dispensed broke the spell.

"Oh yeah, sorry, just thinking." Millie smiled again in Orin's direction, his back was turned as he spoke to Blue, they were both laughing about something.

Jane followed Millie's puppy dog gaze and her eyes widened.

"Millie, you have a crush on someone?" Her voice was stage-whispery and excited.

"No, no I don't, stop it Jane," Millie objected and quickly cloaked at the same time.

"Yes you do! I see the way you look at him, that guy over there with the flick in his hair, what's his name again?"

"Honestly I don't, just leave it, Jane, you know that we don't really fit in. Guys like that don't even know we exist." Millie felt a pang of

70

guilt and tried to usher her out of the hallway but Jane wouldn't let it go.

"Millie, you can't let a load of bullies make you think that you are not beautiful, we've been through this loads of times. We know we're not cover girls but we're the most gorgeous geeks in the school... right?"

Millie looked at the floor.

Jane linked arms with her and continued talking. "Come on, Millie, don't let it get to you, if you have a crush on a guy then that's a good thing."

She hadn't finished her sentence when Jane stepped forwards and spun Millie straight into Orin.

"Oh God, I'm so sorry," Jane said, looking embarrassed.

Above her incessant and embarrassed wittering, Millie heard Orin loud and clear.

*That will teach you to be cloaked! See, I can sneak up on you.*

"Anyway, me and my friend were just going, but she has a cell phone if you ever wanted to talk, I mean its smashed up at the moment but she's gonna get another cell phone, and you guys could swap numbers and..."

"Jane, it's fine, take a breath for God's sake," Millie snapped and Orin smirked.

"I'm just trying to..." Jane objected.

"Just trying too hard," Millie spoke in a deliberate tone and gave her friend direct eye contact that meant 'butt out'.

"Ok, well, erm, I guess I'll just leave you to it with, erm... sorry, what's your name?"

"Orin, don't worry, she's safe with me." He smiled softly and for a second his charm radiated towards Jane and she was speechless.

"See you next class," Millie spoke and gestured of Jane to give them a moment.

"Oh, yes of course. Nice to meet you, Orin."

Jane almost skipped out of the hallway, and Millie knew that she would be fighting the urge to look over her shoulder.

"Hey," said Millie and sniggered. "Sorry about Jane, she's a bit star struck that someone like you could come and speak to the geek."

Orin smiled. "You aren't a geek, Millie, you hide because people have treated you badly, I get that."

"You didn't even know I existed before all of this started," Millie mumbled.

"Because you hide away, not because you are not good enough, there's a difference," Orin spoke softly to her. "You've got to start believing in yourself a bit more."

"I know, but it's hard when you've been through so much shit," Millie sighed.

"Well you've got us now, and we believe in you." Orin pulled her in close for a bear hug and she closed her eyes tight.

"That's all in the past now and we've got work to do." Orin released her and held her at arm's length. "Dig deep Millie, we know you can do it."

She nodded and smiled as the bell sounded and Orin asked her to uncloak just before lunch break so he could tell her where they would be meeting.

"I usually have lunch with Jane," Millie objected weakly, she did want to be with them, with him mainly but didn't want to let her friend down.

"Well find her a lunch date then, it's all good practice!" Orin winked and Millie looked away so he couldn't see the fire in her cheeks again.

"See you later, don't forget to uncloak." He joined Blue and Emma as they walked past, and shouted their hellos in Millie's direction.

*Hey guys, see you later,* she thought in their direction and Emma turned around and waved. Receiving loud and clear then.

Millie made her way to her next class among the constant stream of thoughts and feelings that were swarming around her with every step. She turned them down as she slipped into the seat beside Jane, who could hardly contain her excitement.

"Well?" she prodded Millie in the ribs as she probed her for more information.

"Well nothing, he's just a guy," Millie whispered back.

"We both know that's not true, he is not just a guy, he is a handsome, good-looking and interested guy…"

To Millie's relief the teacher walked in and started to talk about atoms and electrons whilst drawing circles on the board.

*I wish I could meet a guy.*

Millie heard Jane and her heart felt sad, she knew how hard it had been for her to fit in here, coming from another state and into a town where the majority were so small-minded. She'd been picked on from the word go about anything and everything, and the happy, bubbly girl that started high school had withdrawn. She had quickly started to tone down her dress sense and accent in order to blend into the background, and avoid the nasty comments that came her way daily.

Millie thought about what Orin had said and a smile crept across her face, would there be anything badly wrong in playing cupid?

As differences in atomic mass were scribbled on the board and the teacher pointed to the periodic table, Millie was scanning the classroom for thoughts and feelings.

There was nothing helpful coming back and with the thought *expand* she could now hear more of the thoughts on the first floor and some on the second. The thoughts were jumbling together and Millie wondered if she could filter male from female and the moment that her intention was considered, it was done. She tuned in to all of the male energy and was nearly knocked out of her seat with ego and bravado, grunts from the football pitch and a conversation in the locker room between two seniors about online gaming filled her senses.

She was about to quit when something grabbed her attention, with the command *closer* she drew in more of the emotion that was drifting into her awareness from the music block. The lyrics that filled her head were beautiful, and the feelings that they were forged from spoke of heartbreak, loss and the need to love again but a fear of being hurt.

*Matthew Ward*, thought Millie, with excitement and the words stopped flowing.

*What the hell*, she heard Matthew think and realized that she'd projected his own name loud and clear instead of just thinking it. She held her breath.

"What's wrong with you?" Jane whispered.

"Oh nothing, just daydreaming," Millie smiled to herself again and locked into Matthew once more. He was strumming his guitar that he carried everywhere, his thoughts were both raw and melodic and she heard him singing in her head.

*Pause.*

Millie saw the pen stop dead on the board and scanned the classroom quickly only to see statues sitting at desks.

*Fast Forward.*

She could see both her and Jane walking towards the music block as Matthew came in the other direction. Millie looked at all of the possibilities and then drew in an image of him chasing sheets of

74

music and scribbles as the wind blew them out of his hand. The next layer of possibilities appeared to her and she saw Jane kneel down and pick up some paper, then hand it to him and their skin touched briefly. Yes that would do nicely, but this was in the future and Millie didn't want to create this moment right now. There was some recollection of a conversation that she'd had with Orin about future programming, maybe this was it? There was only one way to find out. She left the images and willed herself back into her seat in the classroom, feeling something of a soft thud as she reconnected to the now.

The bell rang and Millie told Jane she had something she had to do this lunchtime.

"I'm being dumped!" Jane said melodramatically. "I hope it's for Orin?"

"Well, it kind of is because I'm meeting him but there's nothing in it." Trying to shrug Jane off the scent of a possible crush was pointless.

"I knew it!" she said excitedly and hugged Millie tight. "I just knew it! Where are you meeting him Millie? Tell me all about it!"

"I think outside the music block, but don't get too carried away, there's nothing going on!" said Millie in a more serious tone, which did nothing to quell Jane's enthusiasm.

"Well there should be, I've got a feeling about this, I really have, I just know that love is in the air!" Jane chattered all the way down the stairs and along the corridor to the music block.

"I wish I could meet someone Millie, you're so lucky!" she said.

"Honestly Jane, it's not what you think." Millie felt bad about not telling her friend the full story but how on Earth could she let her know that she was actually not the girl Jane thought she was.

Oh, and by the way I now hang out with three extras from *Heroes*.

"How can it not be what I think? You don't know what I think!"

Millie laughed out loud at the irony.

"Are you making fun of me Millie?" Jane said with a mock angry expression.

"No I'm just thinking that love comes along when you least expect it and you could end up being blown away yourself soon." Millie held open the door.

"Why are we going outside, its freezing and blowing a gale? Where are you meeting him anyway?" Jane reluctantly ducked under Millie's arm and pulled her jacket around herself tightly as they both braved the elements.

"Stop whining, I don't know where exactly but around here I think." Millie saw the scene around her begin to unfold just as she had witnessed in her mind's eye less than half an hour ago. As they neared the music block the wind blew full force into their faces, and Matthew came out of the door with his guitar case on his back. He had only taken five steps towards them and as he reached to pull a scarf around his neck the wind grabbed the paper tucked under his arm and sent it dancing off across the school field.

"Oh no!" said Jane and started to chase the flying white sheets and Matthew did the same. Millie joined in and handed what she'd caught to Jane.

"I've got to go," she said and smiled, as she made to walk away.

*Sports Hall.*

She heard Orin's voice and turned back into the main block, looking over her shoulder to see Jane passing Matthew the papers she'd caught. Although she couldn't hear the conversation between them, Millie could hear that Jane had seen some of the lyrics Matthew had written earlier that day and thought that they were amazing. She could also hear Matthew thinking that he liked Jane's tattoo on her wrist even though she wasn't old enough, and that he found her kind of cute.

Millie was still smiling as she approached the heavy double fire doors, and as she stretched out her hand to push, they both swung wide open and she heard Emma and Blue laughing.

"Saw you coming!" said Blue and Emma yelled, "Open Sesame!"

Orin shook his head and rolled his eyes.

"Hi guys," said Millie and made her way to sit on a bench.

"Hi Millie!" said Emma and came to join her, the boys stayed standing.

The hall was large and sound echoed around it easily, there was a faint smell of sweat.

"How long have we got Blue?" asked Orin.

"About half an hour, then Shrek's coming in to clean the floor," he sniggered.

"You shouldn't call her that!" piped up Emma. "It's not her fault."

"Agreed, but there is a distinct resemblance," replied Blue and they laughed again.

"Ok guys, come on, we need to talk." Orin's tone was more serious.

As the atmosphere changed, Millie found herself feeling something a little like anxiety creep over her, and it wasn't long before she found out why.

"Orin's right, I've seen some stuff that I need to tell you about and it's not pretty." As Blue spoke Millie felt the hairs on the back of her neck start to rise.

"The night of the portal, you remember that we had to shut it down really fast before anyone else saw it?" He paused for acknowledgment from the others.

"Well it seems that we might not have been successful." He cast his eyes down and Millie remembered the panic she had experienced when her hand was grabbed to seal the portal closed.

"What do you mean?" Emma spoke quietly.

"I mean that something got through, something dark," Blue answered her and his voice trailed away at the end of his sentence into something that sounded fearful.

Orin encouraged him to continue.

"I just can't believe that I didn't see it, I thought we were in the clear," Blue mumbled.

"It's ok man, we've been through this, it's not your fault."

Blue looked at him and shook his head. "It is what it is now anyway, we have to prepare."

"Prepare for what?" asked Millie, her solar plexus felt like a washing machine on its spin cycle.

"Prepare for battle, just like it says in the book. We thought we'd have longer to work with you, train you and teach you Millie but there's no time now. It's here and it's happening really soon." Orin looked at her and picked up all of the terrified thoughts that ran through her head in one instant. He walked over to her and sat beside her, his arms pulled her close and he hugged her.

"I know it's a baptism of fire. You're bound to be scared and we are too, but we can do this." He spoke with conviction and Millie quickly checked his thoughts and found that he did really believe that they could be victorious. Emma wasn't so sure and neither was Blue.

"Ok then, you had better fill me in," Millie spoke and Orin got to his feet again.

"Blue?" he asked with his head on one side.

Blue took a deep breath and sighed it out slowly before he began.

"The night that we opened the portal I checked and double-checked that we were safe and that nothing was watching us, but I was wrong. It was on the periphery and it was using some kind of energetic camouflage that I didn't recognize, it blended into the fabric of the woods. Once we opened the portal it must have seen us being upgraded and I think it tried to travel through the Matrix somehow to try and stop us." Blue paused and then looked at Millie.

"I think it's some kind of Shifter energy a bit like you Millie, but not as evolved. It wasn't fast enough to stop the process but this has accelerated things dramatically. They have been waiting for this for a long time, they have been plotting and planning their side of how to infiltrate and take over humanity, and they have known that we would come along and try to stop them. We're on the radar now and they'll come for us soon." Blue looked at Orin, who continued.

"We don't even have a clear idea who's involved or what their plan is yet, we've been keeping an eye on so many different projects all over the world to try and lock into what they are doing but nothing seems to fit at the moment." Orin paced up and down while he spoke.

"Whatever it is, it's going to be big and we'll know soon enough. They will be rushing to get things in place now so that we can't interfere before it's too late." Orin's words hung in the stale air and Millie shuddered.

"How will we know?" she asked.

"Something's going to kick off any day now and we need to find it, Blue will keep checking to see what he can pick up and Millie, you need to be scanning thoughts of people that could be involved and feedback anything suspicious. Politicians, celebrities and regular people too, it's like trying to find a needle in a haystack but we can work together and focus on different areas. Emma, we need you to go back to The Book and re-read the light and dark chapters again, see if you get anything new and let us know." Orin stood still and looked at Blue.

"Three days. There will be something in three days that shows us the way," he said and Orin nodded.

"We need to be alert and stick together guys, this is it, it's why we came," said Orin in a pep talk tone. "Look for anything unusual, whatever you see, feel, hear or even just get a hunch about, we need to look into, no stone unturned."

Millie could feel fear rising within her from deep in the pit of her stomach. As she listened to Orin's words something came back to her, a memory of a dark and malevolent force flying after her when she was in the Matrix. She should speak up but somehow couldn't, after all, this had been her first time in the energy web and maybe this was what always happened. She bit her bottom lip and looked at her feet.

"Millie?" Orin spoke to her directly. "What's up?"

"I'm just scared I think, this is all new to me and you guys have known this day would come for years now, it's only been such a short time for me." Millie could feel that her voice was about to break with emotion, she took a breath and mumbled something about nightmares.

"What?" asked Orin. "You've suddenly started to have nightmares? You mean since you were activated?"

"Yes, I guess so. I mean I've had them before in my life but the ones that I am having now are different." *What's that got to do with anything,* Millie thought after she had done speaking?

"Millie it's got everything to do with it!" Orin approached her now and knelt in front of her as he reached for her hands.

"When you are in a sleep state you are far more vulnerable to infiltration, haven't you heard of Astral Travel?" Millie shook her head and Orin continued. "It's where you leave your body and travel through the Matrix to different times and places, it happens in either a deep meditative state or in your sleep. These dreams that you are having could be the result of someone or something working in that matrix and taking you to some dark places at night. Are the dreams always the same?"

Millie screwed her eyes together tight and paused before speaking about the night terrors that had been haunting her. "It feels like I'm being watched to start with and then the situation and landscape starts to change until I'm running away and terrified, but I can't see who's coming after me. I never get to see who it is, but I can feel that there is danger and sometimes there's a flickering in the corner of my eye, like something blowing in the wind I guess. I can't see it properly though, it's a bit like what I saw when I was undoing the fireworks." Millie drew a breath to continue but Blue interrupted.

"You saw this same thing in the Matrix, Millie?" His tone sounded concerned and she could feel all eyes burning on her, waiting for her to speak.

"Oh God, I should have told you!" the tears came now and she felt Emma's arm around her shoulders as through the sobs she told them what she had seen and that it felt just like what was hanging around in her dreams.

"It's ok, Millie, you didn't know." Emma passed her a tissue and reassured her, and the others agreed. Orin started to pace up and down and run his fingers through his hair.

"Now we know, we can look out for it, I'll make sure that I stay connected to your thoughts at night, if that's ok with you?" he asked, trying to compose himself.

"And I'll keep checking to see if things are changing, so you stay locked on to me Millie." Blue raised his eyebrows slightly, waiting for her response.

"Yes, of course, that's fine, I just feel like such a moron for not telling you sooner. What do you think it is?" She looked at Orin and he didn't need to hear her thoughts to know that she was really scared.

"We don't really know what it is yet, but it will be some manifestation of the Darkness. It seems from what you've said that it's watching and information-gathering..."

"As well as frightening..." said Millie.

"Yes, that will be deliberate to try and put you off going back in to the Matrix and shifting, and to make you scared of working with us. They know that you are our best chance now and they will be trying to throw you by making you scared," said Blue.

"He's right," spoke Emma, "and I know it probably won't help you, but the more afraid you are, the easier it will be for them to find you. You see, energy is magnetic and it attracts like for like. When you go into a lower vibration energy like fear, you will attract lower vibration energy in."

"She's right," said Blue and Emma smiled at him. "You've got to try and not be scared of all this."

"But can it hurt me?" Millie looked at Blue and Orin for the answer.

"I don't think so Millie, you are much more powerful. Blue, what do you see?" Orin waited as Blue's eyes seemed to glaze over slightly and stare into space for a moment in time.

"I see that you're going to be scared Millie, but safe. That's all I get, I can't see what's coming, only that it's going to be here in three days. I see the date on the top of a newspaper and us looking at it, the date is next Monday."

"So we've got the weekend to get through," said Millie.

"We've got the weekend to prepare." Orin spoke in a serious tone now and they sat in relative quiet.

"Time to split," said Blue, and Mrs. Polinski could be heard pottering about in her caretaker cupboard.

"Let's continue this tonight." Orin looked at all three of them for a nod of agreement. "Stay uncloaked, Millie, we need to know you are ok."

*Please don't let it take her* whispered through Millie's consciousness and goose bumps started to rise on her arms. She looked Orin's way and he turned, not wanting her to see the look of fear that was etched on his face.

The afternoon was draining. Although the voices were filtered in Millie's head, they were still there and really distracting. It was also nearly impossible not to think about Orin, and knowing that he could hear her was awkward to say the least. After about half an hour into math she heard him speaking to her directly.

*Millie I know this is weird for you, I just wanted you to know that I have turned your voice right down so I can only hear you if you think loud. You'll have some privacy that way but I will hear it straightaway if you need me.*

*Thank you,* and with that she relaxed a little more. In between the numbers on the board and the voices in her head, Millie dared to think about what it would have been like to kiss Orin for real, and a part of her even wished that he had heard.

## Chapter 11

Millie could hear her father before she saw the truck and she felt her mood crash. He was trying to talk himself up into a good place ready for her to show up, but he was edgy and needed a drink.

"Hey, Dad." She forced a smile as she spoke.

"Hey. Good day?" She knew that he was asking out of obligation and didn't want to engage in conversation so she kept it brief.

"Yeah, good enough I guess."

And as he turned up the radio, she turned down his voice and fought back the tears.

If only someone could help him.

Millie lay fully-clothed in her bed and the sound of the television downstairs started to fade as she drifted off to sleep. First she was with Orin and they were holding hands and walking along a beautiful deserted beach, the wind blew her hair across her face and he reached to tuck it behind her ear. She could feel herself melting, and as his arms locked around her and pulled her in close, she allowed her eyelids to flutter closed and her lips to part slightly in anticipation of the soft kisses that she had imagined. Even in a sleep state it felt real, and the skin on skin contact drew from her a hardly audible gasp as she felt her body surrender to his hold.

Then a flickering. Almost nothing really but a distraction crept in to her awareness, and in her dream she opened her eyes and turned to look. The darkness was hovering as she had felt before, and it darted away but not before she'd seen something that looked like a face. A dark hood covered the head and what seemed like a cape folded over the body. As the black fabric cocooned the stranger, there was a morphing into the background. Something appeared like a vertical slit and light poured through, engulfing the silhouette being. In the next moment the light faded and the gap in the time-space reality was closed.

Millie could feel a scream rising in her throat and in her dream she tried to cling to Orin, but he wasn't there. Fear gripped her and she searched up and down the beach, running away from what she had seen but her feet made slow progress in the sand. She sensed again the dark to the left of her in the long grass of the sand dunes, it darted out of her line of vision when she turned her head to look, and the sky started to turn black.

Thunder rumbled above her and the sea now crashed grey and wild and freezing spray stuck her long hair to her face.

"Orin!" she cried. "Where are you?" And although she couldn't see any more clearly than before, she could feel that the evil force was getting physically closer. "Orin!" she called again but the sound of the storm drowned out her voice.

Thoughts started to stream into her awareness of darkness spreading all over the Earth, humanity being controlled and manipulated into a society that no longer thought for itself. Then a vision of the elite, the puppet masters and the manipulators controlling all the wealth and resources. Even through her fear she could feel excitement and anticipation radiating through, whatever or whoever this was they were really going to enjoy this, then came the most terrifying thing that she could imagine.

The most beautiful man appeared to her from what seemed like nowhere, and through the fog of fear, Millie felt her heart skip and she caught her breath. He was perfect in every way from his chiseled jaw line, dark tousled hair and piercing green eyes. She felt like everything else around her had stopped still, just like when the Matrix had *paused*. He radiated an energy that started to draw her in moment by moment, breath by breath, and he moved *closer*.

*Millie.*

She heard him call her name and she felt her guard drop immediately and her hands fluttered up towards her throat.

Each one of his strides would have been three or four of her steps, and he seemed to hover above the sand as he reached out his hand to her. He licked his lips and raised one brow as his gaze bored straight into her soul.

*NO!*

Millie blinked as she heard Orin's voice somewhere in the distance, and the stranger increased the intensity of his stare and moved closer. She could feel his energy now and the hairs on the back of her neck stood up as she heard his thoughts loud and clear.

*You are so beautiful in the flesh, Millie, I have waited so long for this...*

She felt her cheeks start to color up fiery red, she bit her bottom lip and felt a yearning for him to touch her.

*I hear you beautiful.* His voice carried a smooth velvety tone that felt magnetic, and Millie found herself being drawn into what felt like heaven.

*MILLIE, NO!*

Orin's voice rang out again like a faraway echo that rippled through the fabric of the dream, and she felt something like a memory that left as soon as it crossed her mind, something fleeting that she couldn't hang on to.

*Come to me, Millie.*

The stranger reached out his hand to her and as she made to do the same, a smile started to curl up the corners of his beautiful mouth, and as a lightning bolt split the sky, he threw his head back and laughed. He reached for her wrist and the moment the connection was made fear, hatred and despair coursed through her veins straight to her open heart and she cried out in torment.

She could feel the whole of the collective darkness of All That Is dragging her deeper and deeper into an abyss that was suffocating in its misery. hot tears poured down her face and her screams combined with every terrified and malevolent thought that had ever crossed a human mind in all of their horrific glory.

She gasped for breath and flailed her arms against the swarming. heavy blackness that cocooned around her, it was choking her, from inside and out.

*MILLIE! MILLIE! COME BACK NOW!*

In the distance there was a vague familiarity in a voice that didn't fit the rest, and she could feel her physical body being shaken.

*I can't.*

As soon as the thought was formed she heard the frantic response.

*YOU CAN! YOU CAN, MILLIE, COME BACK!*

She felt fingers wrap around hers in a faraway place, and someone willing her awake.

*WAKE UP, MILLIE, PLEASE WAKE UP.*

And then a sudden gasp of air, and a judder back into the physical world of her bedroom and crying. trembling and Orin holding her close as she shuddered in the darkness and struggled to make sense of what had just been her most vivid nightmare.

## Chapter 12

"It found Millie in her dream and hunted her." Orin's tone was serious and he ran his fingers nervously through his hair.

No one spoke but Millie could hear Emma and Blue's shock and concern.

"I'm ok guys, just a bit shaken."

"What does this mean? I mean is Millie ever going to be able to sleep again?" Emma directed her question at the two boys.

"Yes, of course she is, it's just that we'll have to work out how to stop them finding her.   There will be a way, Blue?"

"There's a way, but stay awake until we figure it out." He looked at Orin and nodded, they would be working on this together.

"So what are we going to do?" asked Emma, "I mean we've got two days now until God Knows What and they're hunting Millie?" The panic started rising in her tone and Blue walked towards her and draped his arm over her shoulders.

"I won't let anything happen to you, or Millie." She looked up at him and swallowed her fear.

"Promise?"

"Promise," he said with conviction and kissed the top of her head.

"How are we going to keep her safe though, if they can get into her dreams?" Emma asked the question they were all thinking.

"I'll guard her when she's sleeping, I mean I'll tune into her and listen to her dreams and I'll be able to wake her up and bring her back if I need to," Orin said. "I'm sorry, Millie, it's the only thing I can think of."

*Oh God he'll know I dream about him.*

Orin looked at her and shrugged. "It's the only way I know to keep you safe."

*I won't spy on you.*

"But what if you can't wake me?" Millie asked.

"Then we do what we just did, I try and wake you by projecting my voice as loud as possible to break your dream and bring you back, and if I can't I have to get to you and shake you out of it, with a little help from my friends of course." Orin tilted his head in Blue's direction and then Emma's.

"What did you guys do?" asked Millie, suspiciously.

"I checked that the coast was clear and that your dad was going to be sleeping on the couch for the rest of the night," said Blue.

"And I looked through the window and moved the beer bottle out of his hand that was going to smash on the floor and wake him up," said Emma, "and then I saw the keys that were in the lock and turned them so that Orin could race up the stairs and rescue you!"

"Oh right." Although Millie had wondered why Orin was there in the middle of the night shaking her awake, the thought was fleeting and overshadowed by relief to be in his arms and not the nightmare he had saved her from.

"So from now Millie, you need to sleep when I am awake and vice versa, we never sleep together." Orin realized the double meaning and sniggered. "You know what I mean."

"Yeah I know," said Millie and she heard Emma thinking *but she'd like to...* and she couldn't disagree.

"So what now?" said Blue. "We still have two days until we find out."

"We just have to wait," said Orin. "We don't know what we're fighting yet."

Millie's whole life felt surreal. They were all waiting for signs of what was to come. Blue couldn't see a definite outcome, he spoke of two paths, one was "life as we know it" and one certainly was not. They were both weighted with equal possibility.

89

None of them had slept much, especially Millie, who was glad to be protected but couldn't relax completely knowing that Orin had access to her innermost thoughts, and many were about him. They sat in their usual meeting place in the woods and watched the flames dance in the darkness, exchanging their thoughts about what might happen next.

"What did you find out from the book, Em?" asked Blue as Emma raised her hand and gently blew wind at the glowing embers. They flared again and as she spoke she flicked her eyes towards a branch lying nearby and it flew into the fire.

"The Book says just what Blue's telling us. There are two outcomes or endings, two pathways that could unfold and it isn't clear which one is going to happen yet." She shrugged and sighed. "There's some stuff in there about there being a fork in the road, a moment in time when things could change direction and that this will be very definite, it will be a conscious choice, a shift if you like, one way or the other. We'll know it when it happens."

"Anything else?" asked Orin.

"It says that there will be a light and dark battle, we know that bit already, but it speaks of trickery and confusion and there's some mention of the Matrix and being able to move up and down timelines. There's quite a lot of stuff about things not being all that they seem and not taking things on face value, as well as some stuff that I didn't understand about formulas."

"What kind of formulas?" said Blue.

"I don't really know, you know how it's written in all of that swirly lettering, and so cryptic, but they look and feel a bit like chemicals or something scientific?"

"It's not triggering anything for me," Blue replied. "Orin?"

"Me neither, but it's all good information. We can look out for anything that comes up that could be a clue." Orin looked at Millie. "You look tired, we should get back and you can have the first sleep."

Blue kicked dirt at the fire and Emma blew the smoke out of their eyes as they made their way back home, edgy and afraid of what might come next.

## Chapter 13

"Hey!" shouted Jane as she ran up to Millie.

"Hey, Jane." Millie waved over her shoulder to her dad and saw his forced smile through the windshield.

"Millie, are you ok? You don't look so good." Jane linked her arm and they walked together.

"I'm fine, just tired. What about you?"

Jane smiled and spoke in a hushed tone. "I think I'm in love!"

Millie giggled, she knew exactly how Jane felt about Matthew, she'd been picking up her thoughts since they met and she was happy that Matthew felt the same way.

"He's dreamy... and I think that he likes me too!" Jane was glowing as she gave details that Millie already knew but appeared interested in anyway, and when she started to squirm Millie let her off the hook graciously.

"It's just that I'll be spending more time with him, and I hope that's ok with you? I mean we're still best friends and all that, I just want to..."

"Jane, it's fine, I want you to be happy and he seems like a nice guy." Millie hugged her and Jane hugged back.

"Really? You think he's ok?"

"He's more than ok, as long as he treats you right he's good with me."

"Thanks Millie, I just don't want you to feel abandoned."

"I don't, I want you to be happy and I've got plenty on my plate at the moment."

"Your dad?"

"Yes and other stuff"

"I know what you need!" Jane said with conviction "A girls' day out!"

"No Jane, really I haven't been sleeping well, my dad..." Millie's excuses hung in the air and Jane interrupted.

"Your dad just said he'll be back late when he dropped you off Millie, now come on, how long has it been since we went to the mall and hung out together? We can get a makeover and try on shoes and talk about boys." Jane widened her eyes and stuck out her bottom lip in mock petulance. "Pretty please?"

"Well..."

"It's Sunday, Millie! What else are you going to do? Sit around and wait for the world to end?"

Maybe she is a telepath too thought Millie, but a part of her wanted to feel normal again, maybe shopping was just what she needed.

*Orin, I am going to the mall with Jane, ok?*

She thought it loudly, and without waiting for his response, smiled widely at her friend and started heading in the direction of the bus stop.

*Sure Millie, I'm not your keeper but please stay safe.*

*I will.*

"So I want to know ALL about Orin," said Jane as they shared nachos with cheese and chili.

"Well there's not much to say really," said Millie in between bites.

"Come on, Millie! I know you guys are spending time together and I've seen the way he looks at you!"

"We're really just friends Jane, honestly."

"Millie! He is gorgeous and he follows you round school like he needs to know where you are all of the time, he is so protective over you."

*If only you knew.*

"I bet he is an amazing kisser..." Jane nudged her and waited for her response.

93

"Actually Jane, we haven't kissed yet," Millie mumbled.

"What do you mean you haven't kissed?" Jane blurted out and the table next to them looked up.

"Shush big mouth!" said Millie in a hushed tone. "I mean just that, we haven't kissed."

Jane sat back in her chair and folded her arms.

"Well, what's wrong with him?"

"How the hell should I know?" snapped Millie. "I'm not exactly an authority on guys you know, not like you now you've got Matthew!"

Jane looked hurt and Millie apologized, she sighed and momentarily held her head in her hands and then looked at her friend again.

"I really don't know Jane and it's killing me. Sometimes I think he does like me but he makes no kind of move at all, and he does this thing with my hair, tucks it behind my ear and he looks at me and I feel like my heart's going to jump out of my chest. But the only time he leans in for the kiss I'm waiting for is in my imagination. I just don't get it, maybe geeks aren't his bag after all."

Jane's hand reached for hers and she spoke softly.

"Millie I had no idea, I'm sorry for prying. It's just the way he looks at you at school and the way he holds you and ruffles your hair and you laugh together, I just thought that you two were very much together. Maybe it's my fault, I've been so into Matt that I haven't spoken to you in an age and I've put two and two together and made five."

"It's fine, Jane, really. I'm sorry for snapping at you, like I said, I haven't been sleeping." Millie pushed the nachos into the middle of the table and drank the dregs of her Coke through a straw.

"Hey, it's fine, we're good," said Jane checking her watch. "It's time we went though."

"Oh yes, I have no idea what I am going to get!"

"You should go for a whole new you," said Jane as she left a tip.

"Nothing too drastic!" replied Millie and finger-combed her fringe. "I don't want to scare him off altogether."

"He'll love it," said Jane and they made their way to the new hair salon that had just opened with a half price cut and restyle offer.

It was so good to feel normal, thought Millie as she sat in the stylist's chair, a head full of foils and the latest gossip magazine on her knee. Jane had been right, this was exactly what she had needed, and as she flicked through this season's must-have handbags and onto shabby chic furniture up-cycling, an article about philanthropy caught her eye. It was so heart-warming to see successful people giving back to the world, and by the time she'd finished reading about the young millionaire whose company had invented the first super multivitamin and was selling it in the United States in order to fund shipping it for free to the Third World, the timer went bleep and it was her turn to be washed and rinsed.

As the warm waves massaged her scalp and Joanna idly made chitchat about holidays this year, she found her mind wandering and her thoughts wondering if she could use her Shifting to create massively positive events in the world, like rain in Africa.

Millie had turned down her receptors as soon as she and Jane got onto the bus, so many people in one place was such a barrage of information that she couldn't cope. So it was back to plain old conversation and so far, so good.

After half an hour of snipping, the heat and sound of the hairdryer filled her senses and Millie closed her eyes. She knew that she was falling for Orin, but she also knew that she had to toughen up and if he didn't like her then it was hard lines. But something nagged deep within her, sure she didn't have much experience but she wasn't stupid either. He had looked at her *that* way, and he did hold her a split second too long when he hugged her in tighter than a friend. Maybe he was just super protective because they couldn't do it without her, could he be keeping her on side and stringing her along emotionally so that she wouldn't leave them?

"All done." The stylist broke her train of thought and stood behind her with a mirror.

"Wow, Millie!" said Jane. "You look amazing!"

"It's not too much?" Millie sat forwards slightly and scrutinized her reflection.

"It's fabulous!" said Jane. "It really suits you."

Millie turned her head from side to side and the long layers moved with her, giving her hair body and bounce as the colors she had chosen glowed rich browns and coppers. She had to admit that she looked a million dollars.

"Makeover next!" said Jane as they made their way to another floor and took a seat on high swivel stools and waited for their turn.

"Don't you feel better already, Millie Moo?" laughed Jane.

"Yes I do indeed and there is no way I can call you Plain Jane now!"

*Are you ok Millie?*

As she heard Orin's voice loud and clear in her head, Millie jumped.

"What's wrong with you?" Jane stared.

"Oh erm, nothing, I just got a fright that's all."

"Fright? What the hell are you on about, Millie? Jane laughed and shook her head.

Millie forced a smile. "I know! What a moron, I don't know what came over me, sorry."

*Fine! I'll let you know when I am back and when I need to sleep.*

*Ok.*

She suddenly felt a longing to be with him, and she zoned out of the conversation that was going on around her about mineral powders and extra-long lash mascara. When Millie was handed the mirror she had to look twice, she'd always used a bit of blusher and lip gloss but had never been "made up" properly. *I guess that's your mom's job and her mom hadn't been around for a while.* She looked amazing, like herself, but with a side order of fabulous.

"We have to go out for dinner," said Jane. "We aren't wasting our amazing new look!"

"But we ate nachos," laughed Millie.

"That was an age ago, and anyway, it's nearly five."

"I have to get home for my..."

"Your dad said he would be late, remember! We'll head back towards home and we'll get off in the high street and catch the early bird special at The Bistro, come on you know you want to, and it's my treat."

"Ok then, it's a deal."

*Closer to home and closer to Orin.*

Millie glared at Jane when she ordered two glasses of house wine, and felt Jane kick her under the table.

"We look old enough!" she said in a stage whisper as the waiter walked away.

"Jane! We could get into big trouble!" Millie hissed through her teeth.

"Aw Millie, live a little! We're going to be legally old enough in a few months anyway, what's the difference?"

The drinks arrived with the most delicious pasta and Jane swirled spaghetti around with her fork.

"So are you going to tell him how you feel?"

"Oh God, I don't know Jane, I think I'll just leave it for now."

Millie had sipped the wine and it felt cold and acidic in her mouth. She'd forced down the first mouthful along with a flashback of being sick down the toilet a few weeks ago. She forced herself to take a larger gulp and followed quickly with a mouthful of bread, it wasn't so bad that way.

"I just don't get it, I mean he clearly likes you."

"Well not enough to make a move." Millie hadn't realized how hungry she was, and the carbonara here was to die for.

"I can't work it out Millie, the way he looks at you..." Jane's voice trailed off as Orin echoed through Millie's mind, he seemed far away for some reason, or muffled, like she was listening underwater.

*Don't drink Millie, it messes us up.*

"A bit like that guy over there." Jane leaned in and flicked her eyes to her left.

"Who? Where?" Millie drained her glass and looked sideways.

She could feel her face flush as the guy sitting at the bar looked at her, raised his eyebrows and smiled.

Millie immediately averted her gaze and looked down at her clean plate, mumbling "Oh my God!" to Jane.

Jane giggled. "Maybe you should put Orin out of your mind for the time being."

*Millie don't drink anymore, I can't lock on to you,* moved through her mind and erased itself just as quickly as it came, and as Millie dared to look back and notice the stranger's beautiful eyes, lips and physique, she clearly thought the word *cloaked* and smiled back.

The conversation changed to a movie they had seen last month, and they laughed in all of the right places, aware they were being overheard. Millie flicked her hair occasionally and laughed a little too loud, and Jane mouthed updates like, *he's watching you,* and *no wedding ring.*

The waiter approached their table with the dessert menu and to their surprise a bottle of champagne.

"We didn't order this," Jane protested.

"It's a gift, ladies, from the gentleman at the bar," he said whilst using a starched white cloth to polish the two champagne flutes and then to give him grip to twist the cork.

"Oh wow! That's amazing!" said Jane and looked in his direction. "Thank you, that's really kind of you."

His voice stroked Millie's ears, and every word felt like it was wrapped in desire for her in that moment.

"It's my pleasure, something special for two very special ladies, now don't tell your boyfriends."

"Oh, Millie's single," Jane blurted out, and although Millie feigned irritation, she really didn't mind, she wanted him to know that she was available.

"I don't believe that for one second," he said softly, his stare intense and Millie blushed and raised her glass to her lips, swirling bubbles around her mouth and wondering what it would feel like to kiss him. She could feel the alcohol running through her veins and heightening her senses whilst numbing her awareness to the outside world.

*I want to kiss you,* she thought, and then smiled to herself *uncloak.*

As Jane filled her glass again and the bubbles raced to the top, Millie thought about kissing him again.

He looked at her and subtly licked his lips and closed his eyes as if he were imaging it too.

*You're playing with me.*

*I'd like to...*

*You can hear me?*

*Or maybe it's your imagination...*

Millie smiled.

*I'll have crème brûlée.*

"Waiter, far be it from me to presume, but I think the lady would like a crème brûlée."

The waiter turned. "Madam?" and without taking her eyes off the beautiful stranger, Millie replied,

"That would be lovely, thank you."

"What's going on between you two?" Jane asked, leaning in. "Are you having some kind of secret conversation or something? You keep looking at each other at the same time and smiling?! Have I entered the Matrix or something?"

Millie and the handsome stranger both spontaneously laughed. Jane looked puzzled, and a little tipsy.

"We have to go Millie. It's getting late."

*Don't go.*

*I have to.*

*Will I see you again?*

*I hope so...*

*I want to.*

*Me too.*

"Oh, erm, right, yes we do have to go." Millie was aware that her words were sounding slightly slurred and when she stood up the world started to spin a little.

As he walked over to her it seemed like time slowed down, and only when he reached out to tuck her hair behind her ear did Millie realize she had been holding her breath. His fingers glided across her skin and she closed her eyes momentarily, as his touch trailed down the side of her neck she felt goose bumps explode.

"Can I give you my card?" he asked, and held out his hand to her, as his eyes held her gaze. He placed the card in the palm of her hand slowly.

*Close enough to kiss.*

*Yes.*

Millie wanted the world to stand still, and as quickly as the thought formed in her mind, the scene in the restaurant stopped dead.

She looked around her and laughed, she'd forgotten all about the abilities she had until now, so absorbed in what it felt like to be normal again. She turned the business card over in her hand and ran her finger along the embossed golden letters that spelled out Alex Jackson, CEO.

"Alex Jackson," she said out loud to the silence of the room.

"At your service," he replied and Millie gasped.

He stepped closer, although they had been close already, there was now barely space to breathe and she could feel her heart racing and questions running through her mind.

*How come you're not...?*

*I'm like you.*

*What do you...?*

*Millie, you are so beautiful.*

*But I...*

*I know.*

*Know what...?*

*You.*

And as she felt his arms coil around her and his lips touch hers, butterflies danced deep within. She surrendered to his embrace, kissing him back slowly as he leaned in to her and her back arched. Something surged through her that she'd never felt before, sure, she'd been kissed a couple of times but it never felt like this. An overwhelm of desire, emotion and an electric connection flooded through her being and she heard herself moan softly as he kissed her neck tenderly and his fingers wove through her hair.

"This is crazy," she whispered.

"I know," he whispered back.

She closed her eyes again, and parted her lips as he kissed her mouth oh so softly.

The feeling was one of merging, of melting in to him, like she had known him all of her life. It felt like a reconnection to her destiny, to the person her heart had been searching for.

She breathed him in and looped her arms around his neck, drawing him even closer and feeling lost in the moment that she wanted to last forever.

*It's madness but I think I know you.*

*I feel the same.*

*It's like I've been...*

*Waiting.*

*Yes, waiting... and now you're...*

*Here.*

*What happens now?*

*Come with me.*

*Where?*

*Anywhere.*

*But I...*

*Millie, we're the same you and I. I'll look after you.*

*Orin....*

*He doesn't love you Millie.*

*But you barely know me...*

*I know you far better than you think.*

*But how?*

*I've been looking for you.*

Millie was almost unaware of the tear that ran down her cheek, until he wiped it away.

"I know how lonely you've been and how much you want to be loved Millie, I know about your dad going off the rails and your mom..."

She shut her eyes tight as if to shut out the pain and when she opened them she saw a bright vertical light behind him appear in the wall, like a tear in the fabric of time and space.

"I can love you through it Millie, and I can help you get your life back. We're both Shifters and that means we can bring her back, don't say you haven't thought of it?"

Millie shook her head, she was starting to feel sick now and unsteady on her feet.

"No, no we couldn't."

"Why not? We control the Matrix, Millie, we can rewrite reality, you know we can."

"But it's wrong."

"What's wrong about reconnecting you with your mom and helping heal your dad's broken heart?"

She cried openly now and mascara streaked her cheeks as confusion whirled around in her head.

"Destiny has brought us together, I just know it."

He took her hands in his and walked towards the light now and she followed him slowly, there was not much she wouldn't have done to stop the pain in her soul and her longing to see her mother one more time, never mind the lifetime he was promising.

He stepped backwards, and she felt a breeze caress her face, as his jacket lifted and flapped around him like a cloak.

And then the trace of a memory, like a tendril trying to cling onto something real in order to grow, started to creep into her consciousness. His eyes locked on to hers and he pulled her towards him, towards the gap that he had nearly stepped through.

"Millie, come with me, please. We can find your mother and start over." His voice was hypnotic and the hold he had on her heart was nearly as tight as the grip on her wrists now.

"I, I'm not sure, can I sleep on it? I don't feel so good, I want to go home." She felt panic flicker through her.

The wind behind him tousled his hair and the small parts of the scene that she could see behind him seemed to be getting darker.

"What's there to think about? You know it's all you have wanted for years, I am offering you everything you've asked for."

She felt nervous, but didn't know why and she tried to step away.

"No Millie, I've taken so long to find you, I can't let you go now."

"I just need some time, I'm confused, I don't feel well... I haven't been sleeping." She started to cry now and expected him to soften and put his arms around her, maybe kiss her forehead and offer to walk her and Jane home.

"The nightmares are over now Millie," he said and forced a smile.

"I never said I had nightmares, how would you know that?"

"Everyone has nightmares." He faltered for a split second. "I can make them go away."

*Orin I'm scared, I think I've been stupid.*

She thought as loud as she could.

"He won't come for you, he doesn't want you, you know that."

*ORIN!*

"Millie please, we are so good together, I know you feel it." He looked at her with puppy dog eyes and her heart flipped again, maybe

104

he was the one after all? But the rational part of her knew something was very wrong here and she should go.

"I need to go home, my father will be back soon." She was sobbing now, confused and wanting to give up on all of it. Maybe stepping into his arms would be the easiest thing to do, maybe for Orin too, then he wouldn't be caught up in her mess either.

He promised he'd be there for her and he wasn't, she called on him one more time and the echoes of her own words rang through her mind along with a whole mix of emotions in her heart.

*Come with me.*

He raised one eyebrow and pulled her closer, how could this feel so good and so bad at the same time? Her intuition was in panic overload, yet everything in her that was physically female wanted to be whisked away with him forever.

She took one last look around her at the freeze-frame she had created, and wondered if it would *Restart* it as she stepped into his arms. The moment the thought was formed, she saw Jane look up at her in surprise and heard glasses clinking in the background.

She swirled around and saw Alex standing with the plain stone wall behind him, holding her wrist and looking at her in disbelief.

"Are you ok, Millie? I think I zoned out for a second, I didn't see you get up. You look like you've been crying," said Jane.

*MILLIE I'M COMING.* Orin's words shot through her mind like a bullet.

"I'm ok Jane, really just feel a little lightheaded and emotional, I think it's the champagne, I'm not used to it."

"Let's get you some fresh air," said Alex as he released the grip on her wrist and placed his arm around her waist, guiding her towards the door.

"Wait up, I'll come too, it's time we made tracks anyway." Jane reached for her purse and got to her feet.

The door flew open and banged so hard off the side of the bar that it was amazing it stayed on its hinges. Orin strode into the restaurant like the alpha-male of a pack under threat.

Jane jumped and spilled the dregs of her champagne on the table, as the glass rolled over the edge and smashed.

"You'll pay for that you weirdo!" shouted the waiter.

"No problem," replied Orin in a calm and authoritative tone, never taking his eyes off Millie for a split second.

"She's with me," he barked at Alex and walked over to the pair.

"Is that right?" Alex was about the same height and build as Orin, and as the two of them fronted up to each other, Millie screamed.

"Stop it, just stop it both of you!"

"Let go of her," said Orin through gritted teeth, the muscles in his body taught with anger.

The corners of Alex's mouth started to curl into a smile as he tightened his grip around Millie's waist and leaned in to her, kissing her brow.

Millie looked as if she was going to pass out, and was grateful for him propping her up as her hangover started to kick in early.

"I won't ask you again." It was clear that it was taking all of Orin's self-control to compose himself in that moment.

"Or what?" Alex laughed, and as the sound of it echoed around the near empty room,     Millie felt the hairs stand up on the back of her neck. She hadn't seen it before, he's been so beautiful, so charming and it had felt so right, but this was the sound of the laughter that rang out in her nightmares. The alcohol must have affected her far more than she thought, the room started to spin at the same time that fear started to close its grip tighter.

*Orin I think it's him, the one from my nightmares.*

*I know, Millie, we found out this afternoon, we didn't see him coming for you today though.*

*I wish I'd stayed with you.*

*That doesn't matter now.*

*He's a telepath and a Shifter like me.*

*He's not as powerful as you Millie, you've been upgraded.*

*I'm scared Orin, I feel sick.*

*I know it's the alcohol, it drops your energy vibration too rapidly for you to adjust, it screws up your circuits for a while.*

*God, I am such an idiot.*

*Millie, I need you to focus, I know you don't feel like it but you have to.*

The whole exchange lasted only seconds, as Alex stood waiting for Orin's verbal response, he held Millie closer.

*Stop whispering with him, you're coming with me, remember?*

"Can someone tell me what the hell is going on here?" asked Jane, looking from one to the other.

"We're leaving, that's what's happening," said Orin. "Come on Millie."

"I think she can make her own mind up," Alex sneered.

*Shift things back Millie, before you came here.*

*Orin I don't know if I can, everything feels so foggy...*

*You have to try.*

*I'll try.*

*Go back to before.*

*This morning you mean, before the mall?*

*No just before here... I like your hair, don't change that.*

Alex cupped Millie's face in his hands and looked intensely into her eyes, a confusing combination of fear and excitement coursed through her as he started to lean in and kiss her again. She could taste the danger as her lips parted and his magnetism drew her in.

*Millie, SHIFT.*

"Come with me," he whispered to her at the same time that Millie was thinking *Pause.*

*Orin, nothing's happened.*

"Let me back inside your head Millie, I know you're shielding your thoughts from me," Alex said.

Luckily, Jane's perception of events was diluted with the liberal amount of champagne she'd swilled and although on her feet, she had her head in her handbag looking for her money.

*We haven't got long Millie, try again, and would you mind not kissing him anymore?*

*Didn't think you cared.*

*Can we talk later?*

*Still nothing.*

"I'm not hiding from you, I'm new to this mindreading stuff and I can't switch it on and off quickly yet, and the wine's slowing me up even more."

Just then two figures appeared one either side of Orin, and Millie recognized the silhouettes before they stepped out of the shadows.

"You took your time," Orin smiled.

"Better late than never." Blue took up position at his left and Emma on the right and Alex

started to shuffle backwards.

*She can't shift it back guys, he got her drunk.*


"Should we split the tip?" came a slurred and muffled voice from the bottom of a bag.

*It's not looking good, Millie, you need to shift it back NOW.*

Hearing the urgency in Blue's tone made her start to cry again, and she was hardly aware of the thin white vertical line that started to glow behind her, unaware that is until she saw the horror on Orin's face. She turned her head to look over her shoulder and felt herself being dragged backwards as the line expanded and a portal between realities opened up.

"Millie!" Orin yelled and started running towards her, followed by Blue and Emma, but they barely had time to take more than one step. They saw the terrified look on her face as Millie passed through the veil. Orin's fists pounded the wall and his nose stared to bleed from the impact.

"What do you see? Where is she?" he yelled at Blue, who shook his head.

Orin turned on Blue and shook his shoulders as Jane's voice rang out, "Where's Millie? Did you see her? I can't believe she'd go without me and without leaving her half of the tip!"

"Tell me what you see! You're not even trying!" Orin's voice cracked with emotion and as the waiter came back from the kitchen he shouted,

"Hey you two, break it up! Take it outside, we're closed and you haven't even eaten here! Get out!"

He walked to Jane and ushered her towards the door, "Come on, sweetheart, let's get you on your way."

"I can't believe she dumped me like that," said Jane in Emma's direction and shook her head.

"I'll walk you home," Emma replied and linked her arm, looking back over her shoulder and yelling, "Come on guys."

"It's all my fault." Orin fought back tears as they walked along the high street.

"You're why she left?" Jane asked him.

"Not really," said Emma

"I am, I am why she left. If I'd only told her how I felt about her she'd be here still." He wiped his eyes with his coat sleeve. "Where is she, Blue?"

"Oh I can tell you her address," said Jane.

"Thanks," said Blue as Orin shook his head in exasperation.

"So you really like Millie then? I told her that you did, I've seen the way that you look at her," Jane continued, blissfully unaware of the gravity of the situation. "I told her to just tell you that she liked you so much, to be honest about her feelings and that you would be about yours. You guys are so dumb sometimes, you should have just told her, I mean, she adores you..."

"I think he's a bit upset." Emma tried to rein her in but to no avail.

"Well so was Millie as far as I could tell. Apparently he's been blowing hot and cold with her for weeks and she is so fragile what with losing her mom and the stuff with her dad and those vile bullies at school." She paused momentarily only to draw a breath and then remarked indignantly

"I'll call her when I get in and see if she is ok."

As Jane made her way down her driveway, with the odd sideways step and wobble, she shouted thank you and fumbled in her bag for her door key.

Without warning Jane's voice started to fade into the fabric of the street scene and it looked like she was getting further away. They were floating in and out of the moment, like observers and independent of each other, with so much space around them and the faint memory of what had gone before and some awareness of what could be. And then a pulling, a drag, an undercurrent that sucked them through dimensions and a whistling sound in their ears as hearts pounded and the familiar smell of smoke filled their lungs.

The moment that they collided with the new present moment was the moment that their cell memories were cleared of the possible nightmare that could have played out the following day. It was like they'd always been there on Saturday night at 11:03pm talking about what the next days would bring them, and they seamlessly exchanged thoughts and conversation regarding the danger that ensued.

Millie burst into tears and they all looked at her. Orin jumped to his feet.

"What is it? What's wrong?"

"I, I don't know where to start," she sobbed into her hands and felt Orin's arm around her shoulders, her stomach knotted, knowing that she'd have to hurt him by telling the truth.

"What's happened? Why are you crying?"

"You'll hate me, you'll all hate me." Her voice was muffled through her fingers as they exchanged glances and Blue's eyes narrowed.

"Things have changed," he said. "And they are still changing."

"In a good way?" asked Orin with his arm around Millie.

"Maybe, Millie is going to be able to help us advance much more quickly, she knows who we are looking for."

"You do?" Orin said. "You know who it is?"

"How do you know?" asked Emma. "What happened?"

Orin shot Emma a look that said back off. He could feel Millie trembling.

They waited a few moments until she was more composed, and Orin encouraged her again.

"You promise you won't hate me?" she asked.

"Of course I won't, none of us will, just take your time and tell us what happened."

By the time she had finished, the fire was smoking and Orin walked out of the clearing to get some more wood.

"Is he ok?" Millie asked Blue.

"Yeah, he will be, it's just a mind flip that's all. I mean, all of that happened and then it didn't, if you see what I mean. Once it's shifted back we have no memory of what happened, even if we were involved. But as the overseer you have recall."

"There's something I didn't mention," Millie lowered her voice and Emma looked up.

"When he was dragging me into the void, just before I shifted things back, I could hear you all."

Blue shrugged.

"Ah, so you know." Emma smiled.

"Know what?" said Blue.

"Know that Orin really likes you, and he always has?" Emma nudged Blue.

"Right, yeah, he does."

"Well tell her why he doesn't say so."

"He told me after meeting you, after you freaked out in the cupboard, that he really really liked you and that he thought you could be the one for him. He asked me to look ahead and see if you were destined to be together and I told him not to, that it's risky and that he shouldn't make decisions that way. Things can change." Blue sighed. "But he twisted my arm and I looked, I told him what I saw and I couldn't lie."

Silence fell like a cloak around the circle.

"What did you see, Blue?" Millie asked him and braced herself for the answer.

"I saw that you would choose someone else and break his heart."

They heard Orin's footsteps returning with firewood and hushed their collective tone of voice.

"It's ok, I heard, I should have been honest."

Emma got to her feet as Orin threw the wood on the fire, the air she moved through it made it blaze.

"Come on," she said to Blue and held out her hand. "They need some space."

"You're good 'til about 6am, guys," he said over his shoulder.

"So you know." Orin sat beside Millie, with his eyes cast down to the forest floor. "I feel like such an idiot."

"I think I have the monopoly on idiocy tonight," Millie mumbled.

Orin shook his head. "If I'd been honest with you from the start you might not have..." his voice trailed away and Millie finished for him,

"... kissed him?"

Orin looked at her and the reflections of the flames danced in his eyes as he sighed and closed them for a moment.

*I'm crazy about you.*

When his eyelids flickered open, he saw Millie smiling.

*Me too.*

He gently cupped her face in his hands and kissed her tenderly.

*My heart is going to explode!*

*Me too, I think I love you.*

*Good, that makes two of us.*

## Chapter 14

"Thank God you two got it together!" said Emma.

Orin squeezed Millie's hand under the table at the cafeteria.

"I couldn't have kept it in much longer."

"Looks like we're all coupled up then," said Orin and raised an eyebrow in Emma's direction.

She blushed. "Is it that obvious?" she said in a stage whisper as Blue started to walk over with a tray full of drinks.

"Not to non-telepaths." Orin smiled.

"You've been spying on us?" Emma feigned anger and the sugar shaker tipped as if it was going to spill all over Orin's lap. "Or maybe you'd like salt in your soda?"

"You shouldn't think so loud, especially when you're... you know..."

Emma's face looked like it was on fire as Blue slid into the window seat.

"What's up?" he asked her, smiling and guessing that Orin was having fun with her.

"Nothing, I'll tell you later."

"Tell me now, I don't want to be the one who doesn't get the joke!"

"No I can't." Emma squirmed and Orin and Millie chuckled.

"Ems? What is it?"

She leaned over and whispered in his ear and he too smiled and looked coy.

"He's fooling with you Emma, he wouldn't do that, he's bluffing and you fell for it! You walked right in to that one babe."

Orin shook his head in her direction, "Come on, you know me better than that Emma, but thanks for satisfying my curiosity."

Blue's hand shot out and picked up Orin's drink, as it had started to tip up, seemingly of its own accord.

"No you don't!"

"I wasn't going to empty it all," Emma laughed.

"Well why did I just see him with wet pants and a hand dryer? He's just messing, calm down."

"Ok, I'll play nice."

Emma took a sip through a straw and there was a momentary lull in conversation.

"So what now?" Blue spoke first.

"I was gonna ask you that," Orin said and they all looked at each other.

"Well let's start with what we know," Blue continued. "We know that it's him and we know that he's after Millie. That's because she is our greatest asset, without her abilities we can't win this."

"Can we win anyway?" asked Millie. "I thought there were two outcomes."

"Yes there are two, but we need to focus on the fact that we can create the best one, don't give any time or energy to the other outcome Millie, thoughts are powerful and they can draw in outcomes when we get sucked into fear. I mean, I get scared too. I'm not a superhero, I sometimes think about what if... but I snap out as fast as I can, I think that's how the dark can get to us, it lives on our fear."

Millie shuddered. She had experienced that first and didn't want to go there again in a hurry.

"So what do we have to do?" Emma's tone was serious now.

"We need to find out everything we can about Alex Jackson and start second-guessing what the master plan is," said Orin. "I've started researching him online and here's what I found so far." He reached into his inside pocket and unfolded printed out web pages about a company called Humanetics.

"He's the CEO, it's a family business and his father took a back seat two years ago when Alex was given the reins and from then it's been swallowing up smaller research and development companies in hostile takeover bids in order to drive a monopoly in their sector."

"And what's that?" asked Blue. He'd seen lab coats and packaging in some of the visions he'd had.

"Health and wellness, nutrition and pharmaceuticals. They make hybrid type products that they call 'nutraceuticals', like cereal bars packed out with vitamins and kids' formula milk that's supposed to be full of everything babies need and a whole lot more."

"I've seen that advert, the one with the babies on the trampoline?" Emma commented whilst skimming through the loose paper printouts.

"Yeah, that's it," Orin confirmed and continued, "but what the hell have they got in development that could wipe out humanity?"

"And there was nothing online about new products or anything?" asked Emma. "Can you see anything?" she nudged Blue whist still scanning lines of text.

Blue closed his eyes and was still.

"Actually, I think I can."

"What, what do you see?" Orin leaned in closer.

"You're not gonna like it," said Blue and opened his eyes wide to stare at Orin, and before the thought was formed in his head for Orin to read, he could see the fear in his friend's eyes.

"WHAT?" Orin put his head in his hands as Blue outlined his vision.

"They are saying that it's some kind of super vitamin, one that hasn't been discovered yet and they've been running experiments on it and finding all of these miraculous results."

"But it's fake?" Millie asked.

"Totally. It's a regular cheap multivitamin that you can pick up at any store, there's nothing different or special in the ingredients."

"Am I missing something here?" said Emma. "I mean, so what?"

"They are claiming that it's a miracle product, that this missing vitamin is one that can reverse degenerative diseases, improve IQ, even cure cancer and AIDS. Apparently we've all been getting sick because it's a massive nutritional deficiency and that we've all needed this vitamin to keep us well. They've got an advertising campaign ready to go, showing people that say their cancer markers are now non-existent and their kids are ready for university at 10 years of age."

"Are they actors?"

"No, that's just it, they've been experimenting on people without them knowing."

"I'm lost here."

"The thing is that they are adding something to the vitamin before it's pressed into tablets, something that people don't know about."

"What?" asked Emma as both Millie and Orin looked at Blue and their color drained.

"No way," mouthed Orin and shook his head.

Millie looked shell-shocked. "I saw something about this stuff in a magazine, apparently they want to send it for free to Third World countries."

"It's a massive experiment in epigenetics, they've found a way to activate the junk bits of human DNA that makes you really open to mind viruses. It makes reality more fluid for humans, less rigid so they are open to different ideas and concepts."

"Isn't that a good thing? We all need to be open-minded right?"

"It's not a good thing when they are transmitting the thoughts that they want us to think."

"But how?"

"There's a little crystalline marker that gets into our cells from the compound, it passes through the phospholipid bi-layer and gets into the nucleus where it activates the junk DNA and switches on a kind of receiver."

"We haven't all done advanced biology, any chance of English, Blue?"

"Right, I'll dumb it down for you," he sighed at Emma.

"And for me!" said Millie.

"What it means basically is that the bits of our DNA that we don't use..."

"There's bits we don't use?" Emma butted in.

"Yeah. The bits we don't use are kind of inactive, and no one really knows what they are for. Maybe chasing our food when we were living in caves or something, who the hell knows but they've found a way to activate them."

"So?"

"So these parts of our DNA helix control different stuff in our body, our behavior, whatever. I mean it's a minefield and it's totally experimental. I mean, who knows what the effects could be on humans."

"But why are they switching on our junk?"

"This is where it gets really interesting and really frightening. They seem to have a way of sending out some kind of energetic signal that is picked up by some part of the newly activated DNA, and it influences human thought."

"Mind control?"

"Well yes and no. It's more subtle than that. First of all people won't know that it's happening and they will literally think that they are thinking their own thoughts. Secondly thoughts not only influence what we do, they can also change our body chemistry on a cellular level."

"That's why people said they were cured from disease?" asked Orin, who had been listening intently.

"Probably, yes. They probably sent out loads of thoughts, ideas, whatever they call them to suggest that they were super healthy and that their immune system was functioning better than ever, you can imagine. And that's what has triggered the healing process. It's a big fat placebo effect."

"You mean they thought they would get better?"

"Not thought, *believed.*"

They all looked at one another across the table and Millie could clearly hear the sound of their fear as realization dawned.

"But they can influence thoughts any way they want to right?" she asked. "I mean, they could make people feel threatened and scared, that resources were scare and other races should be persecuted... all kinds of awful things?"

"It looks that way," said Blue. "They can influence whatever they want to, and the possibilities for good or evil will be endless."

"So what now?" Emma asked the question they were all thinking.

Orin sighed, "I really don't know."

"Me neither," said Blue. "But at least we know what we are fighting now."

"I don't know if that's better or worse," said Millie and no one responded.

*Morning*

Millie awoke earlier than usual; she had slept fitfully but strangely better than usual which she put down to tiredness and not having to worry about Orin hearing her dreams. It was a relief that he knew now about her feelings for him and she wished that she could immerse herself fully in them without terror creeping in and the face of Alex Jackson.

*Hey, you sleep ok?*

*Yeah. You get some now.*

*Ok, see you at school.*

*Dream about me.*

*Always.*

Millie smiled and hugged her pillow tight, and as she thought of kissing Orin butterflies fluttered in her solar plexus and she smiled. She was in love and it felt amazing.

The temptation to listen in to his dreams was niggling at her, and as she fought the feeling her father's voice filled her head. She heard his nightmare loud and clear, it was a re-run of the day her mother had left.

*I'm sorry, please don't go.*

*I have to, you know that.*

*I can change.*

*I don't want you to change. I want out.*

*Don't say that! I love you.*

*I love you too, but we can't do this anymore.*

*Please don't go, I'll do anything.*

*I have to and I'll come back for Millie once I'm set up.*

Then the slamming of a door, the sound of a car and a feeling of falling to his knees and breaking.

A guttural sobbing that wracked through every fiber in his body and hers in that moment too, as she remembered the fear and panic she had felt as a child. Millie cried into her pillow and was grateful that Orin was sleeping now, she needed time to process this herself. The thought of Alex and his promise of bringing her mother back crept in and she sighed.

The news broke that morning that Humanetics had discovered vitamin X, the miracle missing link in the evolution of human health and well-being and that they were ready to share it with the world. Television screens showed images of happy, healthy people, families crying tears of joy now that their loved ones had been saved from the clutches of cancer, and old-age pensioners doing t'ai chi. Periodically graphs were shown with share values galloping up an axis, and photographs of Alex Jackson with the text 'Next Nobel Prize Winner' scrolling along the bottom of the screen.

Millie felt goose bumps cover her arms when she heard his voice from the television, as her father flicked through news channels with his morning coffee. Orin had shown her how to cloak her thoughts from specific people only, so that she could shut him out of her head, but as his words rang out in her ears about years of research and development and wanting to change lives and help the human race, she felt her heart start to race and she ran her tongue over her lips. Was it possible to be afraid and attracted at the same time? Her mind said no but her body said yes, and as she stared at his face on the screen, she remembered the way that his touch felt on her skin, and then the kisses.

*Still as beautiful*, she thought.

*Still as dangerous*, Orin shot back and broke the spell.

*I'm sorry, I didn't mean....*

*It's ok Millie, but remember that it never really happened.*

*It did to me.*

*But now it's undone, I'm sorry, I guess I'm jealous, that's all.*

*You don't need to be.*

*Try it from my perspective.*

*I love YOU.*

*For now.*

"Come on then if you want a ride." Her dad picked up his keys and made for the door.

She had waited so long for someone she really loved who loved her back, why was she so confused? Orin was perfect and she'd wanted him since that moment in the janitor's cupboard, and now he was hers so why couldn't she shake the hold that Alex had on her?

"I'm sorry," Orin said as he tucked her hair behind her ear.

"What for?" she said softly, as his feather light touch made her cheek tingle even though his hand was by his side now.

"For overreacting this morning, it's just, well, I guess I'm jealous of him, that's all." He looked at the pavement between them and shuffled his feet.

"You have no need to be, Orin, you know how I feel about you." She reached for his hand and her fingers entwined with his. He looked up.

"I just don't know what I'll do if you don't choose me Millie." He spoke softly and sincerely as the guilt of her feelings for Alex wrapped around her like a web she couldn't escape from.

"Don't Millie, don't feel guilty, you couldn't help what happened." He was trying to protect her feelings even though his own heart felt like it was being torn in half, this was the kind of love she had dreamed of.

He smiled and she knew that he'd picked up on her thoughts, as he always does.

"I don't want to keep hurting you, but I can't save you from it, I can't hide how I feel." Millie felt tears start to cloud her vision and as she blinked them back he pulled her close.

"I know that, and I know that this is a weird situation for us both. I try to give you some privacy, I turn your thoughts down in my head but every now and then you think something that I am instantly locked on to. If you are in danger, scared, or thinking about him, I can't help it, it's like everything else disappears." He held her tight and she felt him breathe in the scent of her hair and then sigh into it as he wrestled with his own feelings as much as she did with hers.

"I get that, I mean that's what happens to me too when I hear you." Millie tilted her head and he cupped her face in his palm. As she closed her eyes and surrendered to his kiss she wondered if he could feel her heart racing in her rib cage.

*Yes.*

They pulled apart, but still just a breath away.

*Space Invader.*

*You love it.*

*I do.*

*See you at recess.*

*For sure.*

*Love you.*

*Love you, too.*

No matter where Millie was or what she was doing, it was never long before the words that Alex had spoken to her crept into her consciousness. They were always just a layer below the surface, a thin film called reality separated them from her like a veil. But she could see through and she knew that she would not rest until she had found a way to bring her mother back. She hoped that Orin couldn't hear the background stream of thoughts she found herself always being pulled back into, the undercurrent of emotion and desperation that was eroding any strength that she may have had to not move heaven and Earth back to the way things were.

She'd imagined it so many times, them all being together and all being happy, the normal family that you see on breakfast cereal adverts and vacation brochures. That feeling of being connected by an unbreakable cord that ran from heart to heart and was hardwired into your very DNA was what she wanted back.

Ever since the accident her father had locked down the doors on the emotional prison cell that he simply existed in. He couldn't be there for himself, never mind his daughter, the weight of the guilt that he lived with every second of every day had been so heavy. Millie had watched it squeeze every last ounce of hope, joy or optimism from his very core. She knew that he kept going through the motions for her, but she also knew at times that he thought he would be better off dead, and when he spiraled into thinking this way Millie had no choice but to cloak these thoughts and zone out the desperation as best she could, praying all the while that he would find a way through.

She had spoken a little about the accident to Orin, in an effort to excuse her father's behavior really. He'd said that there was no need and that you never know how something like that affects a person. Then he had asked how she was, and as the silent tears fell onto the shoulder of his sweater he held her close and stroked her hair. What words could you ever use to describe the nightmare that she had lived through? Mangled? Devastated? Bereft? No descriptive could ever come near to the fringe of overwhelming grief that she'd locked up deep inside.

She'd lost both parents that day, one in a black body bag and one that had been dragged under by the torrent of grief, anger and guilt that raged through him ever since. Drowning not waving.

Her grandparents on her father's side had come to stay and help with arrangements and make casseroles. No one knew what to say, nothing was safe to talk about.

The weather brought up all of the questions about the speed of the car and the rainfall on the road that had affected stopping distance. Conversations about school opened up gaping wounds that spilt out memories of her mother being on the fund-raising committee and the leavers' prom that she had been in the middle of organizing. The doctors, self-explanatory, even though Dad was heavily medicated with sedatives, when the stethoscope came out of the bag or his blood pressure was taken I knew he was thinking that her heart was still.

Much of the time was taken up with a silence that hung around like a fog. It wound its way around your throat every now and them and choked out tears that you may or may not notice, the cuff of your shirt was always damp and it felt like there was never going to be any moment in your life ever again when things started to feel any different.

Hope dried up and shriveled inside of you, the new version of you that is, the hollow one.

The moment that you woke in the morning was the best and worst part of the day.

There is a nanosecond, before you stir into the reality of the room and the sunlight filters through the gap in the curtains that you have forgotten.

Forgotten that she's gone and forgotten the aftermath.

And then two breaths later it hits you full force, like a truck thundering down the freeway with a heavy load and before you've opened your mouth to scream it's hit you.

And if you are really lucky, you might be at the end of a dream, the before kind of dream that's laced with the sweet, happy memories of childhood. Maybe the day that you went to the zoo or a birthday party or baking in the kitchen. And although you want to immerse yourself in this precious and fragile moment, as you reach for it and try to hold it close it bursts like a rainbow bubble that stings your eyes and makes you cry yourself awake.

*We could bring your mom back.*

This was the sentence that kept repeating in her mind, it interspersed every part of her day and night since it had been spoken. Its tendrils helped it to grow in her mind and heart, hooking in to emotion and climbing into every moment.

She just had to figure out how, and think about the time that she needed to go back to.

Before the crash was no good, as they'd still be fighting. If she was going to manipulate time and space to bring back the dead, Millie figured that she may as well go far enough back to undo whatever was causing the fracture in their marriage.

Finding out would mean going back into the Matrix, and although it's not smart to hang out somewhere where you are being hunted down, the lure of being able to make everything alright was shining brightly in the dark.

# Chapter 15

Orin and Blue were huddled in a corner looking serious and Emma bustled in behind Millie.

Millie slipped into the seat beside Orin and he draped his arm across her back, his fingertips touched the bare skin on her forearm and she could feel the hairs stand on end.

"So, things are moving fast." He spoke seriously about the task in hand but Millie's mind wandered as he tangled his fingers casually in her hair and she could feel a tornado of excitement start to rise in her stomach. He turned and looked at her and she felt a flush color her cheeks. She looked down at the table and he smiled.

*Hey you.*

*Hey.*

*Missed you.*

*Me too. You're giving me butterflies...*

"When you're ready guys?" Blue spoke and they both turned their attention towards him.

"Sorry, ok Blue, what did you see?"

"Things are changing really fast," he started. "It's like every time I check there is another outcome or another situation that could come about."

"What do you know so far?" asked Emma.

"We know that they are developing this miracle vitamin and adding Compound X and that it's going to be sold mass market, and we know why. They want to influence the way that people think and then behave, but the new stuff that is coming in is all about meetings and money and different groups of people. It's also far bigger than we thought, I keep getting different countries and nationalities and it's evolving into different cultures in different ways."

"What do you mean, evolving?" Emma asked quietly.

"It's like there is a different energy to it in different parts of the world, I dunno, it's hard to describe. Like Africa is different to Europe."

"Is it just the energy of the different countries and cultures that you are picking up on?" asked Orin.

"No, it's more than that, it's not there yet in these countries, there is a program like a phasing-in going to happen one at a time and this is the planning stage of how it's going to happen and how it will be useful to them."

"So what's the outcome that they are looking for?" Millie asked.

"It's all about controlling what people think, but thoughts are the building blocks of so much in human psychology," continued Blue. "On a basic level thoughts create a change in behavior, they are literally driving us to make decisions about what we want to wear, what we eat, if we buy an iPad, what we post on Facebook, everything, literally everything starts with a thought..."

"Maybe I am missing something here, I don't want to sound like an idiot but why would anyone want to do that?" asked Millie.

"You're not an idiot Millie, you're a good person and you don't get it because you don't think like them." Orin squeezed her hand under the table.

"Think about what Blue just said about behavior, that it can influence all kinds of buying decisions for a start, so who's to say that they might not bring out another product in six months that costs the Earth and then start influencing everyone to buy that?"

"Yes, but it's more than that," Blue sighed and shook his head as if he had the weight of the world on his shoulders. "I've seen logos and letterheads and brown files marked 'confidential', handshakes and high-fives all mixed up with the different countries, climates and cultures."

"That can only mean one thing." As Orin spoke, they all looked up.

He hadn't finished the sentence as fear started to creep in and snake her long fingers around each of them.

"Global domination."

"Oh my God," whispered Emma as the reality of what they were facing dawned.

"I didn't expect it to be so fast," said Millie. "I saw something in a magazine about shipping a free super vitamin to the Third World, but I didn't know it would happen imminently."

"That's it!" said Blue. "Different buying decisions, different countries, different influences. I mean, you couldn't influence a guy in Africa to buy a Mercedes-Benz but you could get a mother to buy formula milk for her baby and then hike up the price."

"Kids buying cigarettes," Millie said.

"And that's just the start," said Blue. "When you can influence what people think and how they behave you could introduce all kinds of cultural shifts."

"Racism," said Orin.

"How people vote, gun laws, child protection, it goes on and on."

"So you mean that the human race would be a whole load of puppets with someone pulling the strings?" asked Millie.

"Yeah, that's what I am saying, but the worst thing is that we would never even know it was happening. When it starts with influencing your own thoughts then you think it's your own idea. It's planting a mind virus that will spread like wildfire and everyone will think that it's just the way things are. No more free thinkers or activists, no one to challenge the establishment, no one to undo it."

"Apart from us," Orin spoke gravely.

"Well now, there's always that."

"Your dad's working late tonight you know," Orin said as they walked down the drive.

"So what are you saying...?" Millie had already decided that she was going to invite him over after school and she knew that he knew this, she'd deliberately thought it as loud as she could the moment that she'd heard her dad say yes to the overtime.

*You know what I am saying.*

"Well if you don't want any company, that's fine by me, I just thought we could watch some TV, fool around a bit, you know." He gave an exaggerated shrug of his shoulders and Millie played along.

"Fool around? I'm not so sure, I don't know what you mean."

"Well don't you want to find out?"

*I'm blushing!*

*I know.*

*Stop it!*

*You ain't seen nothing yet.*

"Ok then, but aren't we meeting the others?"

"Later, after dark. Blue's got some stuff he needs to do apparently, and coincidentally Emma is busy too."

"Must be something in the air!" smiled Millie and slipped her hand into Orin's as they made their way back to her house.

"Can I ask you something?"

"Anything."

"It's about my mom."

Millie felt Orin's arm tighten around her waist as they lay spooned on top of her duvet.

"It's just that I can't stop thinking about her, and well, you know, if I could change things."

"Millie, I don't know." She could feel him run his fingers through his hair even though her back was turned, it was something he did when he was anxious and the thought of Millie going back into the Matrix at the moment was enough to make him shudder.

"Orin, this is my mom we are talking about here! My mom!" She could feel tears stinging her eyes and she turned away from him to bury her head in the pillow.

"I know Millie, I know, I didn't say that you couldn't or you shouldn't, I'm just terrified."

"And I'm not? It's me that he's stalking," she sobbed loudly and Orin sat up.

*But you like it.*

"I heard that!"

"Well, don't you? I hear you thinking about him and it drives me crazy Millie, you've got no idea how hard that is for me."

"What about me?" She sat up now, red-eyed and clutching her hands to her heart.

"What about me Orin? I feel like I am going crazy, I can't stop thinking about him and I know it's hurting you. You can't switch off listening and I can't switch off thinking, but I love you! I really, really do and I don't understand why I think about him, it's like I'm under some kind of influence or something. I hate him and I'm scared but part of me wants more connection, I can't help it."

"I know, I know you can't." Orin's voice cracked with emotion and he covered his face with his hands. "And that's what's killing me and why I can't let you go in after your mom, not yet Millie."

"But you can protect me Orin, I know you can and I'll be in and out." She moved towards him now and he felt her arms around his neck and her tears on his cheek.

"But what if I can't?" He turned his face to hers. "What if I can't keep you safe and he finds you?"

"He won't steal me from you Orin, I promise."

"That's what I am most afraid of Millie, that he might not have to."

Millie gasped as he turned and pushed her onto her back, his strong arms pinning her down and his gaze as intense as the skies before the first flash of lightning. He leaned in closer and his grip on her arms loosened. She closed her eyes and felt his lips touch hers, feather light to begin with and then as she felt the weight of his body merge into her, the butterflies danced in time with her heartbeat, as she kissed him back.

He drew away from her and his breath was short. Then, whispering her name, he buried his head in her hair that had tumbled free, and she found her hands touching the hollow of his back. He kissed her neck and Millie bit hard on her bottom lip as her eyelids fluttered closed and her fingers climbed the ladder of his spine.

It felt like every inch of her body was connecting to him, static was building up on her skin, and his touch tingled through every fiber of her as his fingertips brushed her lips and his mouth kissed her face.

*We can't.*

She felt his mouth curve into a smile.

*I know.*

They lay in each other's arms for what seemed like a long time, but Millie didn't sleep, she wanted to experience as much of Orin as she could.

*Stop listening to what I am thinking.*

*I can't help it.*

*It's ok for you, you can cloak your thoughts when it comes to me.*

*I have to.*

*What do you mean?*

*If you knew what I was thinking you'd run a mile.*

He squeezed her tighter and tickled her ribs.

"Seriously though, it's weird that you can hear me all of the time Orin, it's like I have no privacy at all. It's not like I have anything to hide, it's just that sometimes I want to know that what's going through my head is just for me?" Her question hung in the still air of the bedroom and Orin sighed.

"I know it must be hard but I just can't risk it at the moment, I need to know you are ok."

"Can't you turn it down or something? I mean do you have to know everything like how Jane's boyfriend kisses or what kind of underwear he likes? What my dad wants for tea and which day I get my period?" Millie turned over and cupped his face in her hands.

"I'm going to be ok, the book said so." She spoke softly and his eyes darkened with fear.

"We don't know that." His tone was suddenly serious. "And until this is over I need to stay locked on to your thoughts to protect you, night and day. I try to turn you down as much as I can so that I'm not spying on you, I'm learning to hear emotion rather than words so I can ignore the content and feel the emotions if I need to, that way if you are suddenly in fear or panic then I know quickly."

"Do I do that a lot?"

"Not so much, but I've started to get a little sleep myself now and then doing it that way."

"Thought you were less grouchy." Millie giggled.

"One thing though Millie, I know it's obvious but you have to promise me," he said.

She waited for him to continue.

"Don't cloak your thoughts when it comes to me, no matter what. I'd rather have my heart ripped out a million times than have something happen to you. I know you are going to think stuff that hurts me sometimes, that makes you human and I just have to get over that, but please Millie, promise me."

Orin's question hung in the stillness of the now darkened room.

"I promise," she said. "I will not cloak my thoughts when it comes to you, but you have to promise something too."

"Anything."

"You stop cloaking from me."

"I thought you might say that."

"Fair's fair, Orin."

"Are you sure about this? I mean you might not like what you hear, I have a dark side you know."

"I'm sure," she replied. "It will make me feel a whole lot less exposed."

"You're going to hear all about how much I want to expose you..." He kissed her neck and she rolled further into him.

"Not right now, we have to meet the others," Millie said, although a part of her never wanted to move.

"Yes, I just heard them too."

"Hey," said Blue and Emma smiled as they approached the campfire.

"Have you ever thought about how weird it is meeting like this?" said Emma "I mean in the dark in the forest, in secret, it's like some kind of spooky movie!"

"I'll be the superhero that rescues you," said Blue as threw his arms around her in a theatrical gesture and tipped her backwards.

She squealed and laughed, it was infectious and Millie giggled too.

"Let me go!" Emma wriggled to be free and after a couple of moments Blue started spluttering dried leaves out of his face that Emma had commanded to swish up into a mini tornado.

She landed with a soft thud and he laughed at the look on her face.

"Serves you right!" and then he held out a hand and dragged her up, picking twigs from her hair.

"So what's up?" Blue asked Orin.

"Was gonna ask you the same thing."

The mood started to change as Orin and Millie sat opposite the others and silence fell upon them apart from the crackling of the fire.

"I haven't been able to see a whole lot more," said Blue. "When I tune in things are more or less the same, and there are still two main outcomes."

"So what do we do now then? We can't just sit and wait," said Orin, and ran his fingers through his hair.

"I don't know, could you or Millie not tune into him or something?" said Blue.

Millie's eyes darted towards Orin as he spoke.

"No, not Millie."

"But I could just..." she started to object.

"I said no." Orin's tone was serious. "He's cloaked, Millie, neither of us can get through and even if you could you would have to uncloak yourself in order to lock on to his thought field, and that would mean he could hear you, too. That could blow the whole plan out of the water."

"Right," said Blue. "I didn't get the cloaking thing."

"But we could listen into others though?" Millie asked. "Like people that are involved?"

"She's right, you know," said Blue.

"Great idea, Millie," Emma agreed and Orin looked considered.

"Yes, we could do that and start fact finding that way. We'll need to find out who we need to be listening out for and tune out the other voices, it's not easy but with two of us on the case we should be able to make progress." Orin slung his arm around Millie's shoulders and kissed her cheek. "Not just a pretty face!"

"So why can't he hear us?" asked Emma, something Millie hadn't thought about until now.

"I mean you and Millie are cloaked right, so he can't get into your heads, but what about me and Blue? He could theoretically spy on what we are thinking, couldn't he?"

"Theoretically, yes, but there are a few things in our favour," said Orin. "Firstly, he is not as good a telepath as Millie and I because he has not been upgraded like us, this can have all kinds of issues. For instance I am much better at screening a lot of data now and finding a specific person, and also my geographical range is much better so I can work from a longer distance. My cloaking and projection are better too, all since the upgrade. It's the same for you Millie?"

"It's hard for me to describe, it's just sharper and quicker and, like you said, dial ups become broadband." She shrugged, "I didn't have long before the upgrade so can't compare as easily."

"So he will have trouble finding us and tuning in to us, especially if we are further away from him?" asked Blue.

"Yes, and also he is very arrogant and his ego is so certain that he is going to be able to pull this off, he is not looking at anything other than the fastest route to making it all happen for him. We're just not on his radar, apart from Millie."

Millie looked down at her feet.

"Hey," said Orin softly as he drew her in close again, "I didn't mean anything by it."

"I know, I just don't know why it's all aimed at me all of a sudden," she answered.

"It's not all of a sudden, it was always going to be you," said Emma. "Remember what the book said? That you would come and complete the circle and you would be the light bearer that helped us to defeat the darkness and save humanity."

"Are you sure you got the right girl?" asked Millie, still looking down.

Orin laughed. "Of course you're the right girl, I mean other telepaths did apply but you know I have a soft spot for Walk Ins."

Millie smiled slightly and looked up at him.

"I just feel like a bit of a fail so far, I guess."

"You're not a fail! You're our secret weapon, Millie. We just need to work out what to do next."

"I think the data gathering is the right thing, seeing what the other people involved are thinking and see if you can find out some ideas of timing and strategy," said Blue.

"And meanwhile?" asked Emma.

"We just hang tight and see what they get, I'll keep checking to see if things change and you make sure we haven't missed anything obvious in the book."

Emma rolled her eyes at Blue. "You know that crazy swirly writing makes me cross-eyed."

"Well I didn't like to mention it..." he smirked and she play-punched him.

"So when do we start?" Millie asked Orin.

"Whenever you want to. I find the easiest way is to listen for key words and if they are words that people generally really don't use in conversation or their own day to day thoughts then it's easier to filter them out every now and then, and once you have heard them you can bring the sound closer and closer and listen to the whole internal dialogue."

"Ah, ok, I think I get it. So what words will we be listening for? Super vitamins?" asked Millie.

"No, it's all over the news, loads of people will be talking about it and thinking that it's going to cure their cancer and reverse the aging process, something more specific would be better and we can work faster. Blue, what did you see when you were looking?"

Blue's face looked thoughtful and his eyes glazed over for a second.

"There was a whiteboard, hang on and let me see what's on there..."

"Ok, so there's numbers, like formulas and stuff but the people in the room aren't looking at them. They are opening folders marked confidential. Inside there is an agreement that they have to sign, that's the first page and then underneath that there is a list of countries and companies with the key contact names alongside."

"Give me the company name and the contact," Orin asked as Blue continued to zone out and speak in a monotone voice.

"Global Drinks Inc. David Hill, Magnapharma Colin Hammond, Nutritech Dorothy Miles, they are the first intake."

"What do you mean first intake?" asked Emma as he opened his eyes.

Blue shrugged, "Dunno, that's what it said on the top of the page."

"They must be recruiting more and working in small groups one at a time," said Orin.

"That should help us Millie, we can cross-reference the company name with the name of the person and then Compound X and Humanetics, and so on. It will shortcut things for us."

"Ok, well let's get started." Millie reached for Orin's hand and he held her gaze.

"We can do some together on the way home and I will continue while you sleep."

"You can sleep first tonight if you want to."

"I don't mind, just make sure you wake up early so that I can get a couple of hours before school."

Orin looked at Blue and Emma, "I'll send you what I get."

"And I'll keep looking," said Blue.

"What about me?" asked Emma.

"Read the book!" they all said at once and burst out laughing as she rolled her eyes.

Millie was trying to do what Orin had told her, but her thoughts and emotions kept slipping back to her mom.

Orin squeezed her hand as they walked down the top of her street and the moonlight shone pale and white from the night sky.

"Tell me about her."

"What?" It was as if he had broken a spell. Millie blinked and shook her head back to the present moment.

"Your mom, tell me about her."

"You must know all there is to know Orin, you've been able to read my thoughts for long enough," she mumbled.

"I only know the aftermath, Millie, I don't know the before or what actually happened. All you think about is the way that it's affected you and your dad now." He stopped walking and tilted her chin towards him and the moonlight made her face look porcelain.

"I want to be there for you, to help you," he said and leaned in to kiss her.

*I want to tell you.*

She kissed him back and felt his hands in her hair, as her arms slipped naturally around his waist.

*So tell me.*

*It's painful.*

*I know.*

*Just think it, and I'll hold you.*

Millie buried her face deep into Orin's coat and drew him as close as she could. When she was sure that she could hear his heartbeat, and she could feel him breathing her in and holding her tight, she allowed her mind to start searching for something from the time before.

Orin could feel her body trembling as she unlocked the memories and moments. The images filled his head and the emotions flooded his heart, and he held Millie tight as the combined force felt like it could knock him to his knees. He had never experienced recall like this through anyone else, it was as if these were his own memories, not Millie's.

He was stunned by how much he could sense and feel, and how alike her mother Millie was. It was also strange that the recall was through the eyes of Millie's younger self, the fear that pumped through her veins now coursed through his, as her mother threw clothes into a holdall and screamed at her father that she couldn't do this anymore. He heard her father shout back, and the sounds of doors slamming and glass breaking created the background to her mother's wracking sobs. Orin became aware that Millie was watching the scene from a hiding place, a cupboard at the top of the stairs that was full of towels and blankets, she held a freshly laundered facecloth across her cheeks to catch the silent tears as she trembled in the dark and prayed that this wasn't happening.

She wanted to run out and stop her mom, beg her to stay, plead with her to reconsider, tell her that things would be better and that she would do her homework and chores on time. She had never seen her mother so angry and upset and although she was desperate to run to her and hide in her arms and feel her long hair wrap around her, she was rooted to the spot and unable to shut out the scene that was unfolding.

*Maybe she'll get a towel and then she'll see me and tell me to come with her.*

A glimmer of hope.

*Or maybe she'll be furious because I'm hiding and spying.*

Millie sobbed hot tears into the cloth and fought for breath, panic started to choke her and she began to feel dizzy. Her mother's footsteps thundered past her and down the stairs, and she heard the car engine roar to life. Millie flung open the cupboard door and gulped in deep breaths of her mother's scent, running into her bedroom and hammering her fists on the window pane.

Her mother couldn't have heard her, but intuition made her turn her head in Millie's direction. Hesitation darted across her expression and she turned the key and opened the car door. Both feet hit the graveled driveway and her shaky high-pitched voice rang out, "Millie, honey, come downstairs, you're coming with me."

"Like hell she is!" shouted her father and her mother jumped back in to her seat.

By the time her father had stumbled his way up the drive with a bottle in his hand, the sound of the four-wheel drive was becoming distant, but Millie was sure she heard her mother's voice shout out that she was coming back for her later. Her father fell to his knees and let out a heart-wrenching cry, followed by choking sobs that ripped open Millie's heart and made her scream for help.

She ran into her bedroom and started to throw clothes into a pile, tipping the contents of her backpack into the corner, shaking and crying and praying to God that this would stop.

"Please, please help us, please help us, send the police, God, or the angels, or my gran..." She repeated this over and over whilst throwing underwear, a soft toy, homework and trainers into the bag until it bulged full. She forced a nightdress into the lining before fighting with the zip with one hand whilst pinching together the two sides with the other. Her hands were visibly shaking when she reached for her toothbrush, and the sound of the breaking glass in the washbasin made her jump.

"I'm sorry, I'm sorry, I'm sorry," she cried and tried to pick up the pieces and drop them into the small stainless steel pedal bin.

A tiny prick and then her hot dark red blood was spilling into the white sink and mixing with her tears, the room started to spin a little and she reached for toilet paper.

She wrapped it neatly and deliberately around her trembling index finger and continued to pick up the toothbrush to pack, it squeezed through the hole just below the zip and was swallowed into a floral fabric knot. Millie jumped when she turned around to see her father in her doorway. She knew it was him only by the sound of his voice and the smell of the whiskey on his breath; physically he looked like someone different. He was hunched over and looked shorter somehow, his face contorted into a million painful fragments of memory that were visible below the tear tracks and red rims of his eyes. He was dirty. His knees and his hands, and some of the dust from the driveway was sticking to his wet cheeks.

"Millie, honey..." he choked out the words as he stumbled towards her and she instinctively backed away.

"You're afraid of me?" his voice softened and he reached out his hand.

"Where did she go?" shrieked Millie, "where is mom?"

"She's just having a break honey, a little time out, a vacation..."

"I heard you shouting, both of you!" Millie couldn't calm down and the fear and anger combined into a volcano of truth within her.

"Where is she?" she wailed, "I want my mom!"

"Millie, honey, calm down..."

"I want my mom!" She stamped her foot hard on the wooden bedroom floor and started to punch her pillow. The toilet paper bandage flew across the room and blood splattered her face and the ceiling.

Her dad walked towards her and caught her arms in his, and as she flailed and cried, he held her close and cried too. She eventually surrendered and soft sobs filled his dusty shirt as her father rocked her and his own tears fell into her hair and onto her shoulders.

"When is she coming back?" Millie eventually asked in a muffled and defeated voice.

"I don't know honey," her father replied and held her tight, "I just don't know."

"Why did she go away?" Millie asked and her father's words caught in his throat.

"It's grown-up stuff Millie."

Then in the distance they heard the wailing of a siren and Millie pulled away.

"It's the police, I knew they would come!" She ran to the window and looked as the noise combined with another, but remained distant. "I wished for them and they have found her and they are bringing her back!"

She turned to her father and smiled wide and fake, wanting to make herself believe that this was the case.

"It doesn't work like that, Millie, they don't bring people back like that," he muttered, closing his eyes and shaking his head.

"They do! They do! I have seen it on the news before, it's called a missing person and the police find them! That's why I wished for them." Tears flowed freely and incongruently across her cheeks and alongside her smiling mouth.

"But she isn't missing Millie."

"Yes she is! I don't know where she is and so she is missing!" Millie spat at her father and ran over to him to pound his chest with her fists.

He let her hit him until she collapsed in a heap on the bedroom floor, he hardly felt the physical impact over the emotional torrent that was pulling him under. He dropped to his knees and curled around his quivering daughter, pulling the tight ball of her into his chest and cried with her. For the first time in a long while he found himself praying to a God he didn't believe in, to undo what had been done.

The sharp knock on the door jolted him awake and he wondered how long he and Millie had been lying there. She sat up and rubbed her eyes as he made his way to the window to look down and see who was there. Neither of them had heard the sound of the police car driving over the gravel, and one of the two officers that stood on the doorstep knocked again.

"She's back!" said Millie and bolted upright ready to run down the stairs.

"Not yet Millie, just let me see who it is," he answered, trying to control the panic that was rising within him. Had she told them that he'd swung for her? It was an absolute one-off and he had meant to thump a hole in the wall the size of a soup plate but she'd moved and his fist had brushed the side of her cheek by mistake. It had sent her flying and no amount of begging or pleading or apologizing was ever going to make that right. He could blame the drink, or his temper, or the fact that she said she was leaving, but none of that would stack up if she had gone to the cops with a shiner. He'd have to admit it and hope that she backed him up that it was a complete accident and that it had never happened before. Judging by the way she had gone to them and reported it though, it wasn't looking good.

He looked at himself in the mirror at the bottom of the stairs before he opened the door, and hardly recognized his reflection. It was classic of the life that he was now leading, fitting actually. He had no idea who he was becoming, but he knew he didn't like it.

He took a deep breath and opened the door, registering the emotion on the officers' faces as pity rather than blame, and he felt momentarily confused.

"Mr. James Brown?" the man said.

"Can we come in please? I'm Sergeant Jake Milano and this is Officer Jennifer Olson."

Millie's father stood back and opened the door wide allowing them access and gestured towards the front room.

"What can I do for you both?" Millie's father asked as they looked at him through sympathetic eyes.

"You are the husband of Elizabeth Brown?" Sergeant Milano spoke in a measured tone, professional some would say.

"Lizzie, yes, I am her husband, what is this about?" Millie's father may have sounded defensive at that point, God knows he'd had enough for one day and his head was pounding now and he needed another drink.

"We're here with some bad news sir." The woman spoke now and the cops exchanged a quick glance.

"It's your wife," Milano continued "she drives a red four-wheel drive registered to this address?"

"Yes?" He was irritated now. Why didn't they just cut to the chase and tell him she had been down to the station and he was being arrested for giving her an accidental back hander.

"Sir, it's bad news I'm afraid." Milano looked away for a split second in an effort to compose himself and took a breath before delivering the body blow.

"I'm afraid there was an accident." He waited for a response which did not come. "On the freeway about an hour ago. The paramedics tried to save her at the scene but sadly there was nothing they could do. It seemed like she wasn't wearing a seat belt, so the impact of the other vehicle resulted in multiple injuries." He was trying to balance sympathy with the facts and it sounded like a movie script.

No one spoke for a moment, and as Millie's father closed his eyes, his soundless sobs spilled between his fingers and Millie's high pitched screams rang out from the living room doorway, making both police officers jump.

Orin tightened his hold and Millie stood shaking and sobbing into his coat.

For the first time he deliberately broke his promise to her and cloaked his thoughts so that she couldn't hear his own heart breaking, and the vow that he made with himself that no matter what happened, he would find a way to help her bring her mother back.

## Chapter 16

"You look exhausted," said Blue as he and Orin hung around the corridor waiting for Emma and Millie.

"Yeah, you could say that." Orin ran his fingers through his hair and paced a few steps.

"What's up?" asked Blue as Orin looked him straight in the eye and sighed.

"So much, I don't know where to start."

"Try me."

"Let's go outside, they're gonna be a while yet," Blue said, and turned towards the door.

They stood in silence for a few moments, Orin with his back against the brick wall of the technology block, and Blue leaning against the wrought iron handrail opposite.

Orin folded his arms around himself and looked at his feet.

"Don't freak out," he said to Blue.

"What about? Just tell me! What did you hear?" he answered in an irritated tone.

"It's not what I heard, I'll get on to that, some of it's interesting and some not. This is much bigger." Orin's tone made the hairs on the back of Blue's neck stand up.

"It's Millie," Orin continued, "don't freak out, I need your help and I need you to be cool about this." He looked at him in a questioning manner and Blue could see the struggle in his tired eyes.

"What is it?" Blue spoke softly now, this wasn't like Orin.

"She wants to bring her mom back."

"What? Back from the dead? Oh man, that would be the biggest domino ever Orin, you said no right?" Blue waited as his friend looked down again.

"Orin? You told her no didn't you? I mean for a million reasons, you told her no...?" His voice was slightly raised now and he took a step towards his friend who still averted eye contact.

"Orin!" he pushed him against the wall, frustration in his voice and anger in his eyes.

Orin pushed him back. "This is her mom we are talking about, Blue! Of course she's going to want to bring her back!"

Blue took a breath and a step back, shaking his head in Orin's direction. "She can't, you know that. If you have told her otherwise then you've given her false hope."

"There's got to be a way." Orin's words were meant to sound resolute but instead were tinged with defeat. "There has to be."

Blue walked to his friend and bear hugged him.

"I wish there was, it's not only the ethics of it but it's the dominoes that it could set up, it would be crazy and totally uncontrollable." He stepped back but continued talking.

"Ethics? What could be more ethical than repairing a family?" Orin spoke in a confrontational tone.

"And what if by repairing one family, you sacrificed a whole generation?" Blue shot back.

Orin's tone softened, "look, I just need your help."

"Please don't ask me to help you with this."

"If we don't help her I think she'll go ahead anyway," said Orin and they both looked at each other, knowing that this was the reality.

"I saw it all, through Millie's thoughts. I know how she feels and I know she thinks about it most of the time."

"It's that creep that's planted it in her head!" Blue spoke through gritted teeth.

"Yes, he did. But she'd have come to it sooner or later herself anyway, I'm sure of it. All I want you to do is oversee the possibilities that might occur. That's it."

"But to start a new future possibility there has to be a change in the fabric of time and space somehow, you know that."

"I know," Orin sighed.

"And that means that Millie's got to go back in," said Blue as the bell rang and kids started pouring out of classrooms.

"Go back in where?" said Millie as she rounded the corner and linked arms with Orin.

"Hey!" said Emma draping herself over Blue, who kissed her forehead.

"I was just telling Blue that you want your mom back." Orin spoke quietly, with a measured respect in his tone.

"Oh, right. I thought that was between us." Millie couldn't hide her irritation, she knew what the others would think and if they didn't want to help she'd go ahead and do it anyway as soon as this whole episode was done.

"I had to tell him," said Orin, and Millie softened, "we'll need him."

Her mouth became a thin line and she nodded, of course they would.

"Is someone going to tell me what's going on here?" Emma chirped.

"Let's go someplace we can talk," said Orin looking at Blue. His eyes narrowed and then he spoke. "Library, it's closed for those new shelves that they're fitting but the size was wrong so it's empty all afternoon."

They started walking back into school, against the flow of bodies that were heading out for recess, a tide of people that jostled and bumped.

The library was locked. Emma stared past the librarians' desk towards the hook on the wall and in a blink the key that hung there started to jingle its way free and float into the lock. Millie watched as her eyes flicked to the right and the key started to turn in that direction, then a clicking sound and the door swung open.

The air was thick with the smell of paint, and Emma stretched out her right arm. Three windows obediently opened and the cool air wafted in.

"Well then?" she asked.

"Who's going where?"

*You tell her.* Orin looked at Millie.

"I'm going to get my mom back, well, I mean to save her life." Millie's words were a little shaky, but even a lack of confidence could not disguise her determination.

"Through the Matrix?" Emma said in barely more than a disbelieving stage whisper.

"Yes, I'm going back in."

"When?" said Emma, and Orin could hear her loud and clear, thinking what they all were.

*What if something happens and you don't come back?*

"I don't know exactly, when we are done, I guess, and then I can focus better. It's not like there is any rush, when it's changed, it's changed forever." Millie looked at Orin and he could see the paradox of pain and hope in her eyes.

"But what if there's a domino?" asked Emma.

"Or millions?" said Blue, standing with his arms folded.

*HEY!*

Orin projected in Blue's direction.

*It's true!*

"I heard that!" said Millie, fighting back tears, "don't you think I know that? I know there could be a million things that could go wrong but actually, there's plenty going wrong for me at the moment anyway so a bit more wouldn't matter..."

"Millie, they didn't mean it," said Orin as he drew her close.

Blue and Emma looked at each other and an awkward silence descended.

"No we didn't mean it, we just don't want anything to happen to you." Emma reached out and put her hand on Millie's arm.

"Or us," said Blue and Emma nudged him in the ribs.

"I don't want anything to happen to anyone, I just want my mom back and my dad." Millie shook her head and screwed her eyes up tight.

"You don't know what it's like for me."

Blue sighed and relaxed his stance. "Look, I'm sorry. We're all stressed out and tired and I overreacted. Let's say we'll look at how it might work once all this stuff is out the way?"

Millie nodded and Emma smiled at Blue.

"Ok, thanks," Millie said, and Orin nodded.

"We'll all help you, we can find the best moment in the fabric to be able to make a change that will help to save your mom and not create too much universal havoc." He lifted Millie's chin and kissed her, wiping the tears away with his sleeve.

*Ok?*

*Ok.*

*Good.*

*Orin?*

She looked up at him again.

*Thank you.*

*Anytime. I'm on your side.*

*I'm glad.*

Blue and Emma walked over to one of the desks that had been pushed up against the back wall and draped with a dust sheet. They pulled out chairs and the other two joined them.

"So, what did you guys find out last night?" Blue asked when they were all sitting down.

"You must have done the nightshift, you look wiped out."

"Thanks," said Orin sarcastically.

"It was something and nothing really, I can tell you David Hill from World Oil thinks his wife is too fat and is recruiting for a secretary but will only consider applicants that are under thirty, single and with a knockout figure. He is interested in the Humanetics project because he's planning an insider dealing share racket for close friends and family then a swift exit from the company and the face of the Earth with either Mindy or Angela from his current shortlist." Orin looked at them, drew a breath and continued.

"Colin Hammond from Magnapharma is a bit more of a family man but not enough to accept his gay son yet, but he wants to. He is looking at ways of growing the demand for a cancer prevention drug by making people think that they need it, but it has an addictive chemical component in it that will make the body crave it if it's withdrawn with awful side effects. So they are looking at mass distribution, addiction and then a price increase."

Blue nodded at him to go on.

"Nutritech make kids' stuff that tastes like a treat but its chocked full of vitamins and stuff to make them healthy, it's like stealth nutrition that parents sneak into lunchboxes up and down the country. Dorothy Miles feels super uncomfortable with the whole project, but she is also scared that if she doesn't get involved then someone else will, and they will create something really terrible…" Orin finished and they all exchanged worried glances.

"So what's next?" Emma asked what they were all thinking.

Orin shrugged and sighed.

"I honestly don't know what we can do here, I think the only thing we've got in our favor is that it's at the planning stage."

"It's also phase one," said Blue, "So we need to rumble it now."

"Before it starts," Millie added.

"It's already started in some ways," Orin continued. "They have done some small scale trials to see how humans would react, after they did extensive animal experiments."

"Humans? Where?" Emma shook her head.

"It was Dorothy Miles that gave me the heads up there, she was really affected by the way they experimented on a group of indigenous people somewhere out in South America. They took some kind of aid or food parcels out with them that were laced with the stuff and then they started to influence the way that they thought." Orin cast his eyes down for a moment and they all knew the gravity of what he may have seen.

"And that obviously affected the way they behaved, with each other and with the general population. Some of the thoughts they changed were subtle, like wanting to hunt in a certain area to see if they would all comply, but they gradually scaled up the thoughts to really test Compound X and its effects." He was trying to be informative but also vague enough to protect them from the horror of what he had seen.

Millie started to cry.

"I'm sorry," Orin said and pulled her in closer. "I forgot for a moment you could hear it all."

"We've got to stop this," she said in a hushed tone laced with fear.

"We've at least got to try," whispered Emma as she squeezed Blue's hand and looked at him for answers.

"But where do we start?" said Millie.

"With distribution," said Blue. "We have to make sure that it doesn't get out there in the first place."

"And how are we going to do that?" said Millie.

"We have to stop each member of the first intake one at a time," said Orin.

"Blue?"

Blue closed his eyes for a moment and they waited.

"There are possibilities there for that, yes. But it won't be easy," he said. "I don't have a whole load of detail yet but I do see that there are different outcomes now and there weren't before."

"You'll probably get more on each one as we start to focus," said Orin. "Can you see who's first?"

Blue zoned out again briefly and then said, "Dorothy Miles is the one to go for, she's in fear, so she is the one most likely to cave and they'll be able to manipulate her more easily."

"Ok then." Orin looked at Millie. "We focus on her for now, still have an awareness of the others and keep checking in on them, but we go for her first."

"What are we going to do to stop her?" Millie asked.

"I'm not sure yet," said Orin, and they all felt the weight of the task ahead bear heavy on their soul.

## Chapter 17

"We need to get right inside of her head," said Orin. "Find out as much as we can about her and then we can work out how to stop her. Blue, can you keep looking ahead with a focus on possible future outcomes with regard to Dorothy and Nutritech, as well as the big picture."

"What about me?" asked Emma.

"We are going to need you on the ground, to actually put things in her way, I think," said Orin.

"Ok, so let's start with where we find her." Emma pulled out her cell phone and started to Google for Nutritech Head Office and Dorothy Miles' home address. She cross-referenced with Facebook and Linked In, and within moments she had a photograph and full contact details.

"Nice work," Orin said to Emma.

"Now Millie and I need to really focus on what she is thinking about this whole thing so we can find a way to sway her away from doing a deal."

"I'm on to her now," said Millie "She's hungry."

"Yes, me too, salad or bagel?" said Orin and they both smirked.

"Oh she's vegetarian!" said Millie in a surprised tone.

"And has thought about becoming vegan but loves cheese..." commented Orin.

"Ok you guys, we'll leave you to it," said Emma, standing up.

"As interesting as this is..." added Blue.

"Brown or white bagel?" said Millie.

"Well, either makes her bloat..." said Orin and they both laughed.

Blue and Emma shook their heads and made off leaving them to it, with the intention of meeting up again later.

"Seriously, I really don't want to know about this woman's colonic this afternoon," giggled Millie. "Can you listen to that part?"

"No way, that's your watch!" Orin laughed back.

"Ok, ok I guess I'll take one for the team..." said Millie.

"And so you should!" Orin replied and kissed her cheek.

"I'll see you after class and walk you home."

"And I'll tell you all about that colonic." Millie waved as Orin walked away backwards, still looking at her and smiling.

They met after school in a cafe in the high street.

"So what do you guys know?" asked Blue as they all sat sharing two bowls of French fries between four.

"I know this is a whole lot better than freezing my butt off in the woods," said Emma, slurping a Coke.

"Agreed," said Millie and giggled as Emma quickly looked around before the salt cellar seemingly tipped itself up and sprinkled.

"I know way too much!" Orin looked at Millie and she giggled again, he had squirmed when she gave him the running commentary from the colonic therapist.

"Well you said listen in carefully..."

"I don't want to know about nozzles and warm water, thanks..."

"Yuck!" said Emma. "I'm afraid to ask what Dorothy does for a hobby."

They all laughed at the thought, until Blue brought them back into the present.

"So? Seriously. Do you know anything useful?"

"Yes, yes we do. Apart from all of that we found out some stuff that could help us," Orin said and looked at Millie who took over.

"Dorothy is a person that is really invested in helping others. She raises money for charity in her spare time, she supports the homeless and vulnerable children mainly, but she also loves animals and is vegetarian."

"She's really uncomfortable about the proposal that has been put to her as part of the first intake, and actually it turns out that the profilers might have got her wrong," said Orin.

"Profilers?" asked Emma.

"I heard her thinking about some kind of questionnaire thing she has to do online, it was packaged up as a compulsory management training thing and it looked just like it had come down from the top with all of the branding and everything..."

"So they chose the type of people they wanted in this first intake?" Blue asked.

"It seems that way, yes. They looked across industries to get the most spread of influence with different types of consumers and demographics, and then they looked for the biggest players in each sector. Then I think they narrowed it down further by sending out this profiling tool to see who would be the easiest to work with." Orin shrugged, "some of that is my own theory and not necessarily fact."

"It feels right to me," said Blue and Emma nodded.

"So what I heard today was that Dorothy felt guilty," said Millie.

"What for?" Emma asked the obvious.

"She didn't fill out the online assessment herself."

"Oh right!" said Emma. "So they thought they were getting someone totally different?"

"Correct," said Millie. "They thought they were getting someone that was easy to influence if a massive financial gain was involved, the person that filled out the profile was hungry for power and money and they didn't have a great deal of compassion or empathy showing in their personality. They want people that are ruthless, that are willing to stamp on others for their own gain, they don't want people that care about the world and humanity like Dorothy."

157

"So who filled it out then?" asked Blue, sitting forwards with his elbows on the table and reaching for more French fries.

"She asked her assistant to do it, she'd forgotten about it and was overseas with the deadline looming seeing a potential new manufacturer and she had no reliable Internet access. She called her right-hand man and asked him to fill it in rather than miss submitting."

"Wowzer, does she realize how different they are to her?" asked Emma.

"She hates working with him but he is one of the other director's kids, so there is an obligation, and also an understanding that he will be taking his father's place in years to come when he retires," Orin chipped in.

"I bet Dorothy's not looking forward to that!" Emma finished off her drink and the straw slurped the bottom of the glass.

"Not so much." Millie reached over to grab some fries and continued talking. "Anyway, she is not who they think she was when they recruited, and because of that we can probably influence her to walk away from the project."

"But don't they know that she's having doubts?" asked Blue.

"Yeah, I mean he can read minds like you two, can't he? He must be able to hear that she's wobbly about it," Emma said.

"She is definitely on his radar, but he is arrogant enough to think that he can win her over," Millie answered.

"So what can we do?" asked Emma.

Orin ran his fingers through his hair and sighed.

"That's the question really. We need to make her walk away or agree to help him and then not follow through, something like that. She is the link between him getting Compound X into the nutraceuticals that they ship worldwide."

"Won't he just replace her?" said Blue. "I mean, won't they just go back to the list they made initially and look for someone else?"

"Yes, he might do that, but even if he does it will buy us some time," replied Orin.

"I guess so," said Blue, not sounding entirely convinced.

"What have you seen?" asked Orin

"Some of it's good and some of it's bad," Blue said. "But that's better than what there was before, which was all bad."

"Well that's good, right?" said Millie.

"Yeah, it's good. It's just still there that it could all go in the wrong direction. I don't want to give us all false hope, that's all." He looked away for a moment.

"What have you seen?" Orin raised his voice a little and Millie and Emma stayed quiet.

"I've seen the end," he said "And it's not far away."

Millie lay in Orin's arms in the darkness of her bedroom, neither of them wanting to talk about it, in case it drew in the outcome that they feared most.

*I'm scared.*

*I know.*

*Are you?*

*Yeah.*

*What's going to happen?*

*I really don't know Millie, but it's up to us.*

*I love you.*

*I love you back.*

*I won't leave you.*

*God I hope not Millie.*

"Wait, I hear her." Millie sat upright and the moon shone through her window onto her face.

"Me too," said Orin and then they both listened with astonishment at what Dorothy Miles was contemplating.

"We've got to tell the others." Orin spoke excitedly.

"Are you just going to project?"

"Yeah, I'll tell them both you keep listening to Dorothy."

*Hey, Blue can you look at the outcomes with Dorothy Miles? We've just heard her thinking about taking delivery of a load of Compound X and getting rid of it. This one's looking easier than we thought.*

"Ok, they know and Blue's going to see how that intention changes the future possibilities."

"Right, nothing new here."

"He's just firing back now," Orin said and Millie tuned in to Blue.

*There's been a new outcome opened up, looks like she could take herself out of the equation with this one, but there's also something else... there seems to be another far worse outcome. I don't get it, but it's like this decision could make loads of things right or loads of things worse.*

Millie and Orin exchanged glances.

"What does he mean?" she whispered.

"I don't know, but we have to take the chance and hope she follows through," Orin said quietly.

Millie didn't answer but Orin heard the fear welling up inside her thoughts and he pulled her into him.

"Hey," he said softly. "We've got this."

"You believe that?" she said and looked at the way the pale light from the window highlighted his jaw line. Millie reached out and touched his face lightly, drawing a line down his cheek. He turned his head and kissed her fingertips.

"I believe that," he said and as he kissed her, she felt her fear subside a little.

## Chapter 18

The next day at school started like any other day, but by recess things started to change fast.

"What is it?" asked Blue and they all hung around in the corridor near the vending machine and Orin paced.

"I don't know, I can't put my finger on it but something's changed. I only had a couple of hours sleep and when I awoke I did a quick sweep of anyone that I needed to listen in to, and when I got to Dorothy Miles something had changed."

"Like what?" Blue put his hand on Orin's shoulder, "and would you keep still already?"

"I really don't know, nothing obvious or concrete, nothing I can put my finger on."

"Let me take a look" said Blue and the familiar faraway look graced his face for a moment.

"Ah right..." he said when he came back, in drawn out syllables.

The others looked at him quizzically.

"The outcomes have changed, it's not looking as good as last night." He looked at Orin. "You're right, something's up."

"But what?" Orin paced again.

"It's like Dorothy might be on board after all." Blue shook his head. "You said she was different to the profile of people that he wanted."

"She is, at least she was." Orin looked confused.

"That's it," said Millie. "He's shifted something, she's the same but not the same. I bet he got wind of her reservation to stay on task with Compound X, and he somehow shifted something to change her opinions and beliefs."

"But what?" Orin stood and ran his fingers through his hair.

"Something to make her more hardened, less compassionate..." Emma's voice trailed off into her thoughts.

"Does it matter what?" asked Blue. "We just need to change plan."

"It matters," said Orin, "because Millie can shift it back."

All eyes fell on her now and she shook her head. "I don't know what to change, I can't just go in and hope that I get the right thing." Her tone was edged with panic.

*I could bring mom back.*

Orin strode towards her and grabbed her elbows, pinning her arms to her side. "No Millie, No! I've told you I'll help you, we'll help you when this is done, we promise, but not now." His voice cracked with emotion and Millie choked back tears.

*I just want her back.*

*I know, I do too, but not yet, please Millie...*

*You don't know...*

*I know this is killing you.*

*I just want my mom back and I could bring her back, anyone would do the same.*

Orin enveloped Millie and she sobbed. "I'm sorry," he whispered, "I'm just stressed about all of this, I will help you find your mom, we all will." He turned to Blue and Emma, and saw that Emma was fighting back tears too. "Right guys?"

"Right," said Blue, and Emma smiled, not trusting herself to speak without breaking down.

"I'm sorry," said Millie.

"No need," said Orin. "If anyone should be sorry it's me."

He kissed her forehead and tucked her hair behind her ear.

"I think I know what might have shifted," said Millie, "for Dorothy."

"What are you picking up?" asked Orin.

"Fear, can you feel it?" Orin stood still for a moment and his eyes looked into the distance.

"Yes, I can. It's like she is suddenly scared of being hurt or something," he said.

"By Alex if she doesn't comply?" suggested Emma.

"No," said Millie. "This is something that has been with her for a long time, and it affects everything..."

"All parts of her life," said Orin. "At work, at home..."

"But wait, it's changing," said Millie. "It's changing to anger and hatred."

"Who with?" asked Blue.

"I don't know, it feels so general at the moment, like she is mad at the world for some reason," continued Millie, and Orin confirmed this is what he felt too.

"Do you see anything, Blue?" Orin asked.

"Hold on, this is bad." Blue spoke with his eyes closed and his hand on his brow.

"This is really bad guys, she's totally on board and she's going to go for it and as well as that there is some kind of outcome looming that is even worse... as if it could be?"

"What?" said Emma "What on Earth could be worse than this?"

"I don't know exactly, maybe it's too far along the timeline or maybe it's just a slight possibility for now, but it's there - lurking." Blue shuddered.

"What do you mean *really bad*?" asked Orin cautiously as Blue opened his eyes.

"I mean The End," said Blue and they all looked at each other. "The Darkness wins, the end of everything good. I don't know the detail but I know that was the essence of it, and I don't know what the hell we can do to stop it."

"Look, it's just out there as a possibility," said Orin pacing again. "You said it's on the fringe of what may or may not happen so we have to stay focused here. His tone was rising and the panic that he was fighting started to radiate from him, and they all felt it.

"It's always been a possibility," said Emma. "We know that from the book." She reached out to Blue and he pulled her in close, protectively.

"And there is another possibility - that it's going to be ok." Orin spoke but without conviction, the fear of defeat weighed like a dead weight on his mind.

"What's changed?" he asked to no one specific. "What could have shifted her so far the other way?"

"I could find out." Millie's words were slow and tentative.

"Millie," Orin began to object.

"Orin, I have to go back into the Matrix in order to shift back whatever he has done." She touched his shoulder and tried to reassure him. "I'm going to be in there anyway."

"But I wanted you in and out Millie, as quick as possible, I can't have you hanging round in there." He held her tight and she could feel his heartbeat.

"I will be, it won't take me long, I promise." She tilted her head and kissed his cheek, then turned his face to look at her. "I'll be fine."

"You don't know that." Orin's words were loaded with the fear from his worst nightmare, that Millie would be hunted down and he would be powerless to protect her.

"It's our only chance," she replied, and as Orin heaved a sigh and tightened his arms around her, Blue spoke.

"I'm afraid she's right."

# Chapter 19

That night they sat around the campfire surrounded by forest sounds and a tension that made it hard to speak up. They knew what was coming, and they knew it had to be so, but the monumental task that lay moments away for Millie was dangerous beyond belief.

Once she had paused time and space and stepped into the Matrix, Orin couldn't help her. This was different to being stalked in a dream. When he was awake he could hear her, the thoughts in her mind and the screams that rang out in her bedroom.

He could shake her awake, back into the here and now. When she awoke in the present moment, there was no hold over her, it was a case of damage limitation and drying her tears.

But this was oh so different. When Millie froze time, Orin became part of that statued landscape. He was held in the same limbo land as everyone else until she commanded that things start to move again, and he would have no recollection of what she had changed. He would only know the new version of Now. Such was the power of a Shifter.

This is why there was only ever a handful incarnated at a given point in the history of the Earth. And the gift was usually bestowed to someone of great integrity, someone with a pure heart and someone that would hold the best intention for humanity and our precious planet.

Who knows how Alex Jackson had become a Shifter, maybe he had been recruited by the dark side after he'd been gifted with his abilities, or maybe he'd been born bad and a mistake had been made. Orin had never heard of more than one Shifter being in the Matrix at once, and he'd asked Emma if there was anything in the book about it, but there wasn't.

Emma had tried to reassure him and said that The Book was such a comprehensive record of time and space that if it wasn't in there it probably meant that it was impossible.

He had agreed with her in the moment but just because he didn't want to contaminate her with his fear. Just because it hasn't happened yet, doesn't mean it won't.

"What do you see?" Orin spoke to Blue.

"Nothing's changed since earlier," he replied.

"So Millie's right, she's got no choice but to go in."

"I'll be fine," she said, feeling far from fine but trying to gulp back her fear.

"I'll be waiting." Orin said and his stare bored into her soul.

*Come back to me.*

*I will.*

*I love you.*

*I know, I love you.*

"So what happens next?" asked Emma, just as Millie thought *Pause* and the scene around her stopped dead.

Millie took a deep breath and looked around.

The world as she knew it stood still and she could feel her perception growing of the myriad of choices, experiences, people and situations that were the Matrix.

*Now how to do this...*

She thought and instinctively started to draw in closer to the experience in a geographical sense and in moments she had located Dorothy Miles in a freeze-frame, making some toast.

*Now what?*

Millie drew in a breath and held on to Dorothy's energy signature, whilst pulling herself backwards through the fabric of space and time. Snapshots of Dorothy's life flashed into her awareness, boring stuff mainly like work, food shopping, walking her dog. The fear and unrest was evident throughout these experiences, in the background mainly but always there and Millie knew she had to go back to the time before this was created.

She was looking for something that would be coded emotionally into Dorothy's memories as traumatic, upsetting and scary for her.

*Freeze.*

Millie thought as her heart leaped into her mouth and her breath quickened.

*This had to be it.*

What unfolded next was terrifying.

Millie saw Dorothy going through her usual locking up routine at night, feeding the dog and fetching herself a glass of water. She turned the heating onto timer mode and was about to make her way upstairs when there was a knock at the door.

Barney started barking and as Dorothy told him to shush she made to open the front door.

"Who's there?" she asked before sliding the dead bolt.

"I need help," answered a female's voice.

And although Dorothy's intuition told her otherwise, she unlocked and opened the door and was immediately knocked flat on her back.

She awoke in hospital some hours later, feeling disorientated and battered and as soon as she was able, the police took a statement.

They broke the news to her gently that Barney was no longer with us, and when she asked if he had run away with fright they had to spell out the attacker's cruelty.

Heart broken and bones broken, Dorothy spent the next three weeks recovering physically, but no amount of pain relief could help her with the emotional scars.

*No wonder,* thought Millie. This had to be the event that hardened her and turned everything around, making her angry at the world and afraid at the same time. Feeling like there is no justice and wondering why kind-hearted people should give a damn about anyone. Something was taken from her that night and it wasn't going to be returned again without reversing this whole incident.

*Alex did this.*

For his own personal gain he turned someone's whole life upside down and ripped all the goodness and hope away. What kind of person does this? Millie couldn't help thinking that she had seen his true colors, and no matter how charming and magnetic he was, he was evil as well.

*Rewind.*

She thought and the scene ran backwards, up to the point where the man and woman were walking along Dorothy's street talking about getting a fix.

As Millie observed them and looked for possible different scenarios, their image started to flicker. It was as if there was some kind of sticking or slowing down in the Matrix, it only lasted for a moment like when a television channel is not quite tuned in properly and the picture bounces.

*Weird.*

A man came out of a shop doorway and shoved the change from his grocery shopping into his back pocket, and Millie felt the couple think about robbing him.

*Freeze.*

A possible future outcome opened up where he was home safely but cursing himself as he looked through his trouser pockets. Millie drew this closer and saw that minutes earlier, in his haste to avoid the two vagrants on the sidewalk, he had dropped a fifty. It floated out of his pocket and into the eye line of the woman, who quickly swooped on it and started to laugh like a hyena.

Dorothy Miles double-locked her front door and Barney barked at the noise on the street, then he made his way into his basket and Dorothy went to bed.

*Play.* Started to form as a thought in Millie's mind but before the essence of it rippled as a command into the Matrix, she felt herself catch her breath as something moved in her peripheral vision. The outcome she wanted was still ready to activate, and hung in a 3-D holographic form about to burst into reality. She turned around to look behind her and gasped with fright, taking two steps backwards.

"Hey, Millie!" Alex's voice echoed slightly in the vastness of the space that surrounded them.

"What are you doing here?" she cried.

"I was just going to ask you the same thing," he smiled, "but I see that you've come here to undo what I started."

"I can't believe you would take that poor woman's life away like that." Millie could feel terror constricting her breathing and adrenalin racing around her body as she started to second guess what would happen next. She stepped back again, and he stepped towards her.

"I had no choice," Alex said in a matter of fact way.

"There's always a choice," she replied, wishing that Orin could hear what was going on, "and you choose to hurt people."

"Millie, I'm not as bad as you think..." He stepped towards her again and locked his eyes onto hers, and Millie felt herself falter for a moment.

*That Kiss.*

A split second was all he needed and as Millie stumbled to move out of his reach he grabbed her wrist and pulled her onto her feet and into his arms.

"Millie..." he spoke softly as she turned her face away from him. "I don't need to be telepathic to know what you're thinking."

"I'm thinking that you are evil and I want nothing to do with you," Millie said and started to squirm. Was it her imagination or did her response feel half-hearted?

"I know that's not true, I know you have feelings for me." He tightened his grip and Millie felt herself starting to surrender to his hold. There was something about him that connected with her in a way that she had never known before and although she knew in her rational mind that it was so wrong, there was a part of her that felt this was so right.

"I can't stop thinking about that kiss," he said and started to stroke her hair with one hand as the other kept pulling her into him in the small of her back.

"No, I can't do this!" Millie said "I can't it's so..."

"Easy to love you..." and his lips brushed her forehead as the electricity of their touch made her gasp into his chest.

"No, no it's wrong, you're evil, you want to hurt people!" She pushed both her hands against him and tried to step back.

"Maybe you can change me Millie, you could be my savior." He looked almost angelic and Millie felt herself want to surrender to the moment. Maybe the fight was over and this was her destiny after all, whatever came next right now, she felt that she wanted it to be with him. What was happening to her?

It's like he has some kind of hold, he could unravel her with a look and disarm her completely with a kiss.

He cupped her chin, and as her head tilted slightly to one side, he leaned into her and her eyes closed.

Millie didn't notice the fabric of the Matrix starting to change along with her intention.

She didn't feel the ripple that began to morph time and space into another reality, or the future possibilities that were now forming as a result of the kiss that now enveloped her senses.

She allowed herself to fall deeply into the feeling of connection on all levels, her fingers tangled in his hair as he kissed her just the way she had replayed in her mind so many times since the first.

Around her the darkness started to creep in, changing layer by layer the possibilities that once existed, and with that came a wave of dread that collided with the back of Millie's heart and caused her to step away.

"What was that?" she asked and spun around, her vision darting from one side to the other.

Millie's breath was short as he turned her face back to look at him.

"Nothing, we are the only ones here." He leaned in to kiss her again, and the feeling of craving him collided abruptly with panic.

"What's happening?" she said as she pulled away again.

"Millie, nothing... please let us be together, I've waited so long for this..."

"But it suddenly feels wrong, I can't explain it." She turned again to look around her and looked for the image of Dorothy Miles going up to bed and her dog sleeping in his basket.

"Where's it gone?" she called and desperately started to try to recreate it in her mind's eye in order to draw it back in.

"See how powerful we are Millie? We've changed the future by wanting to be together..." He had hold of her wrist and she couldn't tug herself free.

"What do you mean? We can't have!" Millie was crying now and as she thought about the idea that future possibilities had been changed, different images flew through her mind.

"No! No!" she shouted as pain and destruction filled her senses.

She saw the rich growing richer and elitism thriving with the select few that controlled industry, education, health and humanity. An overwhelm of feelings rushed through her and tears streaked her face.

"Millie, it's ok," Alex said and reached for her. "We're part of the rich set, look..."

Millie turned and saw a likeness of herself standing with him, laughing and toasting their success, knowing full well that the way they had arrived there was by destroying the lives of others.

"That's not me!" she screamed.

"It is you, and it's ok. I want you with me when I'm in the seat of power, your life will be charmed." He spoke like he believed it and Millie felt herself shudder.

*Think, think, think...*

She closed her eyes tightly and drew a deep breath.

*Something good, please something good...*

Surveying the raft of possibilities again as they ran like a ticker tape through her mind, Millie caught an image that pulled at her heart strings. She saw herself and Alex in a couple's embrace, arriving at some social event or other, and in the background stood Orin. He was looking at her with such sadness and such love that her sobs started again, and as Alex said her name and it sounded out all around her, she immersed herself in Orin's energy and his love for her.

*Focus.*

She felt her heart open, and the heavy, dense cloud of fear that surrounded them felt like it was beginning to disperse, then it stopped. She opened her eyes and saw Alex just feet away, laser focused on the image of her and him sometime in the future, the happy couple that ruled the world. His concentration and intention generated something that looked like a heat haze, as sweat beaded on his brow. This was becoming a battle of wills, but she knew since her upgrade that she was stronger, she had to be or this would be over before it began.

*Closer.*

The image she was pulling towards reality was changing, Alex's image didn't look as clear now and a new future possibility was opening up, at the same social event but this time it was starting to feel like she was with Orin. The more she kept her attention on the detail and the feeling, the more it adapted itself to what she was imagining. She didn't dare look in Alex's direction as she sent the last ounce of her concentration towards drawing in this future possibility into her current now time experience and thought *Play.*

Laughter rang out around her and the sun shone bright on her shoulders. Glasses were raised and a toast announced to the happy couple. Millie felt Orin's arm around her and as he turned to ask her what was wrong, everything suddenly stopped.

*Rewind.*

It took seconds to find the man leaving the shop and dropping the fifty again, and as soon as Dorothy Miles' feet started to tread her stairs, Millie was searching for the moment in the forest just before she'd entered the Matrix.

Locking on to Orin's energy she could feel relief starting to flood through her.

*Closer.*

With what felt like a bump she was back in the present with all three of them looking at her.

"Are you going to do it now Millie?" asked Emma. "You suddenly look really shaken, maybe you should wait a moment before you go in."

And with that she collapsed into Orin's arms and sobbed out the whole story.

## Chapter 20

"Let's get you home." Orin kissed her forehead and helped Millie to her feet.

She was in no fit state to argue, she might be able to function on less sleep, but not after an ordeal in the Matrix. It had leeched nearly every drop of energy she had left, and she gladly allowed Orin to lead her back through the woods and to her own front door.

"Fast asleep," said Blue as Orin used Millie's key to let them in, passing her father snoring on the couch with the television flickering in the background.

"Sleep well," said Orin and kissed her again, knowing that he had a long night ahead of watching over her. He wasn't tired yet anyway. After hearing her speak about her encounter with Alex he'd find it hard to come down.

Emma carefully turned the key in the lock on the inside of the door and they made their way across the street.

"Does it look different?" Emma asked Blue.

"The outcome? It's gone back to what it was like before the blip," he said. "Two likely outcomes, one good and one bad but they are both equally weighted at the moment."

"Well I guess that's something, we're back in the game at least." She slipped her hand into his.

"You ok?" she asked Orin, knowing that Millie's recount must have shaken him to the core.

"Yeah, yeah I'm ok," he mumbled.

"You're so not ok," she said, shaking her head.

"I am, really I just wonder..." Orin started to speak and then drifted mid-sentence.

"Wonder what?" Blue asked.

"Really?" Orin stopped walking and looked at them.

"Yeah, why not?" replied Blue.

Orin sighed and looked down at his feet.

"I wonder," and then he paused and his voice was a little louder than a whisper, "I wonder if she'll pick him and not me."

"Don't be silly!" said Emma, walking over to him. "She loves you Orin, she really does, it's obvious!"

"What, so obvious that she accidentally finds herself kissing him whenever they meet up?" he said sarcastically.

"I can't get my head around that either to be honest, but I can see she loves you, I just don't know what kind of hold he's got over her. It's like she gets sucked in or hypnotized or something when she's near him, it's totally weird."

"Yeah. And a whole lot of other things besides." Orin's head hung as if he'd already been defeated for a moment and then he spoke to Blue.

"Will you look for me?"

Blue looked uncomfortable and shuffled from one foot to the other.

"I don't know, I mean what if it's not what you want to hear?"

"Then I'll suck it up and keep going."

"But it might affect the outcome here. I'll have to check that first."

"No worries."

Blue looked thoughtful and then confirmed that it was fine to look. Orin tucked both of his hands in his pockets and waited, clearly concerned about what he was going to hear.

"I'm sorry." Blue spoke in his friend's direction. "I don't know what to say."

"You don't have to say anything." Orin replied as he turned his back on them both and headed for home himself.

*Hey.*

*Hey you.*

*I'm awake.*

*I guessed.*

*You can get some sleep now.*

*Ok.*

*Thanks for watching over me.*

*No problem.*

*Orin?*

*Yeah?*

*I love you.*

*And I love you, more than you know.*

"What's wrong with Orin?" Millie asked Emma as they walked past the gym.

"Oh, I think he's just shaken after last night, we all are."

*Shit!*

"Shit what, Emma?" Millie stopped walking and stood with her hand on her hip.

*Don't think about it!*

"Don't think about what?"

"Erm, nothing, it's a surprise... and we've kind of agreed not to tell you about it..." Emma did all she could to think balloons and flowers but soon lapsed back into her real self.

*She knows I'm lying.*

"Emma! Tell me! What is it?"

"It's nothing."

*It's everything.*

"WHAT IS IT?" Millie could feel tears starting to sting her eyes, was this girl her friend or not? And what the hell could she be keeping from her?

"Alright! I'll tell you, but before I can, you have to do something."

"Ok, what?"

"Cloak so Orin can't hear you thinking."

"I promised him..."

"Just do it Millie, it's only going to take a minute."

"Ok, done. Now are you going to tell me?"

"Don't freak out."

"Just say it!"

"Ok, well..." *God I can't believe I am doing this.* "Last night after we took you home Orin went all quiet and we asked him what was wrong and he said he was scared."

"We're all scared Emma, what else did he say?"

"He said he was scared of something that might happen, something involving you."

"That I'll get sucked into the Matrix and never come back?"

"No, not that."

"Then what?"

"He's scared that you won't pick him."

"What?"

"He thinks you might pick Alex and not him."

"That's ridiculous."

"Is it Millie?"

"Of course it is, you know how I feel about Orin, he knows how I feel about him too. I don't know why he would doubt that."

"He made Blue look."

"No."

"He saw it Millie, and he had to tell him, we can't lie to either of you, there's just no point, you can read us anytime you want to."

"What? What exactly did he see? What did he tell Orin?"

"He told him the truth."

"And what's the truth?"

"That you pick Alex. He saw you lying together half-naked in his bed in some fancy loft apartment."

"That can't be right! It's a mistake! It has to be, there's no way I'd do that."

"It's what he saw."

"Then he's wrong." Millie turned on her heel and started to stride down the long corridor that formed the backbone of the school building with Emma calling after her to wait.

*Uncloak.*

*Orin, where are you?*

*Here, I'm here.*

*I'm sorry, I'm so sorry...*

*It's ok Millie, it's totally ok.*

*I choose you, I really do, I promise you. He means nothing to me.*

*I hope so Millie, but if you don't, I want you to know something... even if you don't, I will always love you.*

## Chapter 21

"Colin Hammond," said Blue. "He's next."

"Ok, we'll stay close to Dorothy Miles, she's back to her compassionate and humanitarian self and wants out of the deal. She's working out how she'll get there, so for now she's relatively safe." Orin squeezed Millie's hand under the table.

"We'll start tracking Colin Hammond and see what we get, I have a free period so I'll start now, Millie has a math test so she needs to concentrate." He raised an eyebrow and looked at her and she feigned shock.

"I told you I've stopped cheating!" she said and elbowed him in the ribs.

"Yeah right!" he said and the others laughed at her blushing.

"Well it's a perk, if I'm going to go into the Matrix and fight demons for us then I think I can cheat a little in math."

"I guess you can have one more cheat then, but mindreading only this time," said Orin and ruffled her hair, but the mood had changed with the mention of last night's happenings.

The bell rang and they went their separate ways.

*Sorry.*

*What for?*

*I shouldn't have mentioned it.*

*It's ok.*

*I'm an idiot.*

*As long as you're MY idiot.*

*Hey!*

*As long as it stays that way.*

*It will. I promise.*

"So here's what I know," started Orin. "Colin Hammond is the CEO of Magnapharma, a pharmaceutical company that has bought up lots of smaller companies over the last fifteen years in a bid to become a giant in the industry. Most of the companies they buy up are for the patents and pipeline drugs that they are working on, they strip out the best staff, usually in research and development and then they spit out what's left. Some acquisitions have been strategic in terms of eliminating the competition when they feel that they could be able to produce similar products for a cheaper price, and so on."

"Right, and he is nearing an age where he wants to retire. He was a founder of Magnapharma and although he's not an old guy, he has worked in a stressful environment for twenty years now and he wants out," Millie added.

"I thought you had a math test!" said Orin.

"Well, kind of... but once I knew what the teacher was thinking, the answers came quite easily." She smiled and shrugged.

"Oh and he hates his son. Well not his son, his wife's kid, he's only been married a few years and he reluctantly adopted Steve as part of the package. He thinks he is a lazy, workshy, good for nothing asshole. His words, not mine."

"I got that too, and the kid is gay which he's got a problem with too," said Orin.

"So he's not exactly tolerant," Emma commented.

"I wouldn't have said so, he's thinking about how to get the kid out of the house before he retires, and he wants to retire on the money he's going to make on Compound X."

"It's a cancer drug they have in production isn't it?" asked Blue.

"No, not a drug that treats cancer, a drug that they reckon *prevents* cancer," said Orin. "Can you imagine that? I mean, who wouldn't want to take something that could help you dodge that bullet?"

"But is it real?" Emma looked skeptical.

"Apparently, according to all of the research they have done in double blind placebo-controlled trials, it's totally true in most people." Orin had been fortunate that Colin had been discussing the trials with his head researcher that afternoon, and the implications for their imminent marketing campaign.

"They can't say that it does something it doesn't," he said. "In order to get the product licensed for sale, they have to be able to show all of the data that they have collated."

"If the data is all true, of course," said Blue.

"There's always that, and quite honestly I wouldn't put it past him to exaggerate and manipulate the results in some way, he's that kind of person. Generally though, I think there has to be an adjudication process or something, someone has to oversee it and agree that the claims are correct before it's unleashed on the public." Orin shrugged. "Anyway, the disgrace of it is that this is not a new drug or compound at all. It's just a simple and cheap vitamin and mineral compound like the ones you can buy in any high street."

"So how did they get the test results that showed it could prevent cancer?" asked Emma.

"They used Compound X," Orin said.

"What?" asked Blue.

"I know, it's shocking, and it's out there already." Orin sounded serious.

"So they gave the people on the trial Compound X in one group, and not the other so that they could influence them to be healthy?" Millie had missed this part, it must have been when she was immersed in algebra.

"I think so, remember it works in two ways. Firstly it makes your thoughts malleable, so they can change and influence what you think by sending out thoughts, ideas and frequencies that you are aligned with and this can change your behavior. So people in the Compound X group were given loads of cues that they were healthy and well and their behavior started to change to be in alignment with this. They started to drink more water, exercise, meditate and such like, because all of these ideas were suggested to them in their environment and subliminally as well as energetically through sending thought forms as frequencies," said Orin. "And I only know this thanks to the convo he had today with the head research guy."

"What do you mean by frequencies?" asked Blue. "I mean, how can they send an idea to someone?"

"I don't know that part yet, but there is some way of transmitting something, and the people that have had the compound can pick it up and it affects them, it's to do with markers and junk DNA and stuff."

"Wow. That's scary." Emma snuggled into Blue.

"I know," Orin continued. "And the next thing it can do is based on the thoughts that you are thinking, you not only change your behavior, you can switch on and off bits of DNA and make physical and psychological changes in who you actually are. This part isn't new, apparently it's been understood in some circles for a while that your beliefs can affect what happens in your body. That what you think sends out signals to cells to react in different ways and this can lead to either good health or health issues, they are just taking it to the next level."

"So what's their big plan?" asked Emma.

"They want to go mass market and global with this cancer prevention drug," said Millie, who had heard Colin counting the billions he stood to make.

"Maybe I don't get it, but would that not be a good thing?" asked Emma. "I mean if people think they are well and then they get well, that really is disease prevention and that's good right?"

"That would be good, but it's only half of the story. The product is going to be launched on an unsuspecting public with a whole marketing song and dance about it being a miracle drug, at a really low price, and even given for free to people on welfare. After about six months of influencing people to feel great as a result of regular consumption of Compound X and sending out feel-good frequencies, people will start to notice the difference. They will feel great and tell their friends, starting a ripple effect, and everyone will be taking this amazing product." Millie looked at Orin who continued with the more sinister details of the master plan they had overheard.

"That's when the game changes. What people don't know is that there is an addictive aspect to the product, something that's been put in to make sure that you succumb to the most horrendous side effects the moment you stop taking it. And it's once they have the general population hooked, that the supply and demand issues start. Less of the product will be available and it will be hiked in price, so the cost of feeling good suddenly becomes astronomical. They will keep sending out all of the feel-good frequencies so that the people that keep taking it will stay well, and therefore keep advertising the product."

"That's evil," whispered Emma "I can't believe someone would do that."

"And Colin Hammond will be long gone, once his shares in Magnapharma have peaked and his exit strategy kicks in."

"He doesn't give a damn about the people whose lives will be ripped apart in all of this, he just wants to be richer than his wildest dreams and be sailing around the world in his yacht drinking champagne."

"So how do we stop him?" Emma spoke and shook her head in disbelief.

"Blue, do you see anything that might help?" asked Orin and Blue looked thoughtful for a moment.

"There's definitely a possibility that it's not going to happen." He drew a breath and sat back in his seat. "I don't really know how to put this..."

"Just say it," said Emma.

"It's really weird though, I mean a bit crazy if you ask me."

"And this isn't?" said Orin.

"Ok, I'll let you have that one. But seriously, one of the outcomes that I'm seeing is showing me him terrified out of his skin and stuff flying around a room. What's that all about?"

Blue chuckled. "It also feels kind of funny."

"God knows! He doesn't seem to be a funny kind of a guy. All we can do is stay tuned in and see what comes up."

"Ok, laterz." Blue stood up to leave and pulled Emma to her feet.

"Your parents are out for another couple of hours, shall we watch a movie at your place?"

"If that's what we're calling it..."

Blue winked at Orin as they walked away and Emma giggled as she swung her bag over her shoulder and grabbed Blue's hand.

"Maybe we should have some time together?" Orin asked.

Millie could tell he still felt wounded and she leaned in to kiss his cheek.

"I'd love that. Just me, you and Colin Hammond."

## Chapter 22

Orin stopped under a tree and kissed Millie on the walk home, and she could feel the recent gap between them close instantly.

"What do you want to do then?" Orin asked. "We've probably got a couple of hours."

"Something fun, something normal. I haven't felt normal for weeks now. I 'm not sure if I ever did, but you get my drift."

They held hands and ambled along the sidewalk making suggestions of what "normal" people might want to do after school on a Thursday.

"I know, eat," said Orin.

"Wow, that's exciting!" said Millie sarcastically, "I said normal, not boring."

"Yes but in order to eat we have to cook!" said Orin, sounding more animated

"Oh I can't cook Orin, I burn soup," Millie objected and shook her head.

"I can cook," he said.

"No way."

"Way."

"What can you cook?"

"Erm... popcorn?"

"That's not cooking, Orin."

"Yes it is, there's ingredients and everything..."

"Butter and corn. That's it. Hardly ingredients."

"Well what then?" Orin slid his arm around her waist and kissed the back of her neck.

"Maybe..." she giggled. "I believe that's called watching a movie according to our friends."

"Or making out where I come from." He spun her around and Millie felt her back touch a fence post as he cupped her chin and looked at her intensely.

"You know it's not just that don't you?" He started to kiss her cheeks and then moved down to her lips. As Millie tried to answer, her voice was breathless.

"Well, I do hope that this is included in the deal though..."

"I'm sure it is." Orin kissed her neck and she felt her body start to surrender to him.

"I don't think we're going to get much work done."

"He's going out tonight with his wife, I heard it while you were mocking my cooking ability." Orin stood back and cleared his throat and Millie smoothed down her sweatshirt as a little old lady walked past tut-tutting with a fluff ball yapping on the end of a lead.

"Maybe we should get back and continue this indoors." Millie's face was flushed with embarrassment and the thought of being alone.

"Great idea." Orin said and took her hand.

After a few moments passed Millie asked where Colin was going with his wife. It turned out that Orin had heard him on the phone to his wife, Janice, making the arrangements. It's something that her friends had organized as a couples' night out and Colin was less than disinterested. He's only agreed to go since Janice was taking antibiotics and wouldn't be able to drink, so he had a ride there and back and could drink the night away while the others bored themselves silly with the most ridiculous entertainment he'd ever heard of - a Ghost Walk. Apparently the old hotel that they were visiting used to be an asylum way back when, and now parts of it had been renovated to appeal to the jet set, but parts of it most definitely had not. He'd suffered numerous psychics coming to the house and even some guy with metal dowsing rods and burning sage at one point. If Janice continued this crap he would seriously have doubts about her mental health, and perhaps his own for staying married to her.

It was her "hobby" and was up there with asking her Angel for a parking space, I mean please. There's either a space or no space, but Colin could tell you for sure that there was definitely no Angel.

"Do you believe in ghosts?" Orin asked Millie, who looked thoughtful.

"I believe that we go home once our Earth life is done, but I think that a part of us can come back if that's what you mean."

Orin regretted bringing it up as soon as he realized that she'd be thinking about her mom again.

"I'm sorry, I didn't think."

"It's ok, really it is. You can't go through your life not mentioning accidents, ghosts, moms..." Her voice trailed off into silence at the end of her sentence and she looked wistful.

"I have learned that I can't expect other people to get it. I mean, when something so massive happens to you, it feels like the whole world should stop. But you see people going about their daily lives, they go grocery shopping, they cut the lawn, they walk their dog and bike to work. It's like you're trapped on the other side of a pane of glass and you can see it going on, but it feels unfair and ironic. It's like they don't know how good they have it and that's the way you had it the day before it happened, but you didn't know either."

Orin squeezed her hand and nuzzled her neck. "I'll do all I can to help you get her back, I promise."

"I know you will," she said, and Millie heard him praying that he could keep his word.

"I'm gonna check in with Blue, hope I don't disturb anything." Orin grinned in a deliberate attempt to lighten the atmosphere.

Anyone else his age would have called or Facebook-messaged but Orin shot through a targeted thought and waited to see what bounced back.

"Millie, it's changing..."

"What do you mean?"

"I think it's since he's arranged to go out tonight, there's a possibility that he's going to walk away from the deal."

"Something must be going to happen tonight then, what do you think? Did you get the name of the place they're going to?"

"Yes, let me think... it was something like Hazelwood Hall, I think."

Millie started to Google on her phone. "I don't believe it, it's not that far. Hold on, the number 67 bus goes right past it, we can get it on the hour every hour from the main street."

"We can't just show up."

"Why not? He has no idea who we are. We'll look him up on Google images and make sure we know it's him and see what happens next. Please Orin! This is so exciting!"

"And what are we going to tell our parents?"

"We'll just say we're at the movies or out for pizza or something, or tell them the truth that we are going to some ghost walk thing, they'll put it down to us just being crazy kids. My dad won't even know I'm gone once he's started to drink."

"Let me think about it for a second, I don't want you in any danger this time."

"I won't be in any danger, you'll have me right by your side. Go on, it'll be fun. Pretty please?" Millie fluttered her eyelashes and revealed a mock pout.

"Ok, leave a note for your dad and I'll see if the others are in."

## Chapter 23

Hazelwood Hall was far from spooky. It was like something from a Scooby Doo movie, with pictures that looked like their eyes were being moved to follow you, and creaky floorboards.

The four of them arrived a little early, and had to sit in the library while Abigail Childs waited until exactly 7:30pm to start the tour.

A car pulled onto the gravel drive and two couples walked towards the main entrance.

"That's got to be him," Millie said as a portly balding man took a drag from a cigarette and lagged behind the others.

"Colin, come on!" one of the women confirmed and he rolled his eyes and nipped the end of his smoke.

"I'm nervous," whispered Emma.

"No need, it's all a big hoax," said Blue.

"I know that!" she laughed. "I mean I'm nervous we'll get rumbled."

"They have no idea who we are," said Millie. "It's exciting!"

Abigail bustled into the room and looked over the top of her glasses.

She clapped her hands and started to speak in an authoritative tone, starting with the date that the hall was built and the wealthy family called Hazelwood that had commissioned the work.

Millie and Orin exchanged glances and fought back their smirks as Colin started thinking about the size of Abigail's ass.

Abigail explained that the family fell into financial difficulty and the hall fell into near dereliction, before it was needed as an asylum. People were brought here that suffered from depression, had children out of wedlock and were generally "simple". Very few inhabitants would have warranted being locked up here, and because of that there were several suicides during this time. These were apparently the ghosts that walked the building at night, and why the last owners of

189

the property had fled and instructed that it be opened as something of a museum and tourist attraction.

The tour began on the ground floor in the room they sat in now, it apparently had not always been a library. Even as Abigail was telling them in a compelling tone that this is where a young mother is supposed to have taken her life, by tying together bed sheets and hanging herself from the rafters of the old laundry, she was thinking about stopping for food on her way home. She mentioned that staff had seen the ghostly figure of the dark-haired woman pacing at night and had heard her tormented cries for her baby that was taken away at birth. The two women's eyes widened and they looked at each other, which was all the encouragement that Abigail needed to ramp up the story even more.

She moved on to the sound of the baby crying for his mother and her making the window panes rattle, while she was thinking *bullshit*, which was exactly what Colin was thinking too.

Abigail wrapped up and started making her way through to the kitchen. Everyone followed but Colin lagged back.

*Let's have some fun*, Orin sent to the other three as they shuffled into the hallway.

Emma glanced in the mirror opposite the reception desk just long enough to see Colin's face as she commanded a book to slide out of place on a shelf, hover in front of his face and then thump onto the floor. He froze, and a scream caught in his throat.

*Don't you believe in me Colin?* projected Millie loud and clear into his headspace and he looked around in terror.

Although all of the windows were tight shut, the curtains started to flap gently at first, but quickly whipped up to a frenzy and Emma smiled to herself.

*Help me Colin! I'm trapped between the worlds Colin and I know you can hear me!* Millie threw at him now and his color started to drain as he staggered out of the room and bumped into Blue.

"Sorry, sorry, I just think I felt something in there...." He certainly looked like he'd seen a ghost.

"Colin, are you alright?" his wife asked from the front of the party.

"Yes, yeah I'm just fine hun." He took a deep breath and said that he might need some air.

"He means a cigarette," his wife said not too quietly.

She was right and the smell of smoke drifted through to the kitchen along with Colin coughing.

He was trying to justify what had just happened with his logical mind, and telling himself to "man up" when Emma started to swing the hanging basket behind him. It creaked unnervingly and as he turned around to see what the noise was she swung it right off its hook and it smashed at his feet while Millie sent him an almighty shriek.

He ran into the house like a bat out of hell, and into the kitchen where Abigail was holding court and talking about the beheading of a member of staff when an inmate had escaped from a straitjacket and got hold of a meat cleaver.

*If they believe that they'll believe anything,* she thought out loud, and a part of her felt guilty about spinning them such a yarn but she knew that the company sent a mystery shopper around once in a while to check she was sticking to the script and her former colleague Nigel sure wishes he had.

Colin's wife was wittering about inmates spending time in solitary confinement and how she couldn't possibly, while they filed out and into the front room. Emma tucked her chin into the collar of her coat so no one could see her smile and she started to shake the knife block that sat on the counter top a little. Colin heard it and turned to look as the tea cups started to dance in their saucers.

There was a cork notice board on one of the walls with pinned postcards and a fire safety notice. Colin gasped as one of the knives swooshed through the air, narrowly missing him and quivered as it flew like a dart and embedded itself into the opposite wall.

*Colin, I know you hear me. You're just like me, bad through and through. I deserved what happened to me because of the darkness that lived inside of me, and you deserve what coming to you.......*Orin winked at Millie as he saw Colin twitching with fear.

"He's begging for mercy and denying that he has ever done anything wrong, he's praying to a God that he's mocked for years to get him out of this," Orin told the others and Emma turned the pressure up.

The kitchen drawers flew open all at once and the contents started to fly around the room.

Colin stood flapping like a maniac as a hurricane of tea towels, dishcloths, cutlery and paperwork swarmed around him from all angles.

*You're next Colin, you're next if you don't bail out on the Compound X deal.*

*We know what you're doing and we know where you live, you can't get away from us Colin, an eye for an eye. If you ruin lives, we'll take yours, make no mistake...*

Millie projected a bloodcurdling cry and as the sound resonated around his mind, Colin fell to his knees with his hands over his ears and started to cry like a baby.

Abigail and the rest of the party rushed in and his wife went to him and knelt on the cold tiled floor.

"Colin! Colin! What's wrong?"

"What the hell's happened here?" Abigail looked around in amazement and irritation, she'd have to get the whole place squared up before she got out of here tonight. What was this joker thinking?

"I don't know what happened... the drawers just opened and stuff flew out and I could hear the voices..." He was wiping tears from his eyes and his wife was trying to dab his face with one of the lone dishcloths.

"What could you hear? Who was it?" his wife asked.

*He's having a breakdown,* thought Abigail.

"I heard both of them, her and him, they were wailing and saying I would be next..."

*Here's hoping, you asshole.*

"Well why don't you go outside for some fresh air, sir and we'll tidy up in here, these spirits can be very active sometimes..." Abigail could do with a smoke herself and she hoped that they wouldn't want to continue after this.

"Outside?" he spat at her, "I went outside and they followed me!"

*We're coming home with you tonight Colin, there's no escape...* sent Orin in his best spooky tone.

*Unless you quit the project, we know what you are doing and it's EVIL, you have to walk away for us to walk away...* Millie joined in and Colin started to wretch.

"Sir, please go outside and get some air," insisted Abigail.

"Come on hun," said Janice, and helped him to his feet.

"She doesn't believe me..." Colin said to her and Abigail smiled sympathetically and thought    *no I bloody don't, you douche bag.*

Emma and Millie were gathering up the debris and filling up the drawers again. Orin dislodged the knife and replaced it in the block while Blue zoned out for a moment to check what could be coming up.

"Looking good," he said as Abigail ushered the two couples outside. "Well good and well, nothing really..."

"What do you mean?" said Millie.

"I mean there's one future possibility that looks positive, but the other is literally nothing when I ask what he's going to create, or what tonight's changes will influence."

"Let's hope that's all good then," said Orin. "I'm ok with a good and a nothing, whatever that means."

"Me too," said Millie, and they started to make their way out.

Abigail was filling in paperwork and they passed her relatively unnoticed, down the steps and onto the gravel driveway.

Colin's wife was apologizing to their guests who were saying it was fine and totally unexpected, and could it be something he'd eaten. Colin was having one more smoke before he got into the car; his hand was shaking as he lit up and took a drag. As they walked past him Emma saw a dead bird on the lawn that looked like it had been savaged by a cat. As he paced back and forth trying to compose himself, she made its dead and lifeless body flap its way under his feet and as the bones crunched along with the gravel, he whimpered like a girl.

*Get out of the Compound X deal, we're watching you.*

Orin sent him loud and clear and he slipped his hand into Millie's and they made their way back to the main road.

## Chapter 24

"Do you think we went too far?" giggled Emma.

"I know we scared the living shit out of him but we needed to really, I mean the fate of humanity rests on what these people do next. And quite honestly, he couldn't care less about what happens to the little people. He knew full well that lives would be filled with fear and families would be ripped apart, and all he could think about was himself," Orin said.

"I know, it's for the greater good, but it still feels horrible scaring someone like that," said Millie. "But it was kind of fun!"

"We can't think like that," Blue said. "We need to stay focused on the task in hand, time is running out."

"What have you seen?" Emma asked what they were all thinking.

"Nothing new, there's just a feeling that it's all very close." Blue shrugged.

"How close?" asked Emma.

"Days," said Orin as he looked at Blue and picked up the word that flashed through his mind and transferred in a blink.

They had thought their work was done for the night but with Blue's latest insight, Orin felt compelled to start eavesdropping on the third would-be supplier. David Hill from World Oil was watching TV and drinking Scotch when Orin tracked him and started listening.

His wife Cilla was hiding in the kitchen scoffing a family bag of potato chips that she thought no one knew about. She knew she'd gained a few pounds, but she had to eat regularly because of her thyroid, at least that's what she told herself and others as she waddled down the aisle in Wal-Mart filling up on her guilty pleasure, Fat Food. She cooked every night, a dinner brimming with all things good, but it was when David was settled in front of the box with a drink in hand she retreated to the kitchen to 'clear up.'

Clearing up meant more than just doing the dishes - she crammed thousands of calories into her mouth in between scraping the plates and loading the dishwasher. The ironic thing was that David knew full well what was going on. He knew where her stash was, and he knew that she hid the wrappers at the bottom of the trash. The truth is he wasn't bothered, he'd disconnected years ago and was treading water to find a way out of this. He had hoped that she would eat herself into an early grave, but that could be a good few years to go with her secret troughing. And he knew what he was missing, there was plenty of eye candy where he worked and in his position, with an eye-watering bonus every year and a company car that cost the equivalent of most people's life savings, he could have his pick.

He could divorce her, but the headache and financial hangover would be horrendous, two kids meant that she'd get the house and a monthly income until they were out of college and more than half of his hard-earned lifestyle stash would be swallowed up in alimony.

Sure he loved his kids, but they were teenagers now and wanted little to do with him unless they wanted their allowance. He was pretty sure they wouldn't miss him in between the obligatory school holiday access visits.

Compound X came just at the right time for him, he'd have more than enough to pay Cilla off and launch his exit strategy, with whoever his new PA ended up to be. They thought they were being recruited to keep his diary in check and fetch his cappuccino, but he wanted the personal aspect to be far more personal.

He'd want some female company on his round the world tour, and although it may only be a temporary position, he knew that the criteria included a knockout figure, an aim to please attitude and someone that was easily impressed with his cash. He didn't want any more kids so that would have to be sounded out early on, and there was certainly no chance of getting married again. Out of the frying pan and staying that way, thanks.

The ice cubes clinked in the glass as thoughts streamed through his mind and straight to Orin, who wanted to know more about the detail of his distribution plan.

He didn't have to wait too much longer as David's mind wandered to the type of yacht he was going to buy and how much it would cost, he mentally started to stack up the shareholding that he had at the moment, along with his bonus and expenses and multiply it in accordance with the anticipated supply and demand issues that were coming up in his master plan.

It was during a discussion with Colin Hammond from Magnapharma that the penny had dropped. David knew that his marketing team were just about to push the button on a massive campaign called Well Water, the advertising was all mountain streams and people doing yoga and the clinical trials had been massaged to show that by ionizing water you could create all kinds of health benefits for young and old. They were after the Evian market and so were targeting the same demographics as them, with the same marketing messages and then some. A cheaper price point and a money back guarantee were all part of the bargain. The finance director though he was crazy and went on a rampage about returned stock and refunding monies, saying that it would be a logistical nightmare. He was of course correct, if this was actually going to happen. David knew that once he had people buying Well Water at a knock down introductory price, and the frequency started to transmit from Humanetics HQ that they not only felt great but needed to keep feeling great, that sales would be solid. There was none of this baby coming back and he knew it. Granted, he didn't have the addictive component like Colin Hammond in his anti-cancer thing, but who wouldn't get addicted to feeling good? And anyway he just needed one big hit, a cashing-in process and he was out of here.

What happened next had nothing to do with him, but one thing was for sure, no matter where he ended up in the world he wouldn't be drinking Well Water, and he'd make up some story of contamination to keep his kids away from it as well. As for Cilla, she'll have to take her chance. And anyway, it was unlikely she'd waste precious trolley space in the supermarket with bottled water when there was room for potato chips or Oreos.

Orin mulled over what he had heard. The profilers had done a great job in choosing David Hill. He didn't seem to have an ounce of compassion for anyone else including his wife, who Orin could hear thinking about how low she had felt for years and how desperately unhappy she was.

She has suspicions that he was having an affair and was terrified that she'd be left destitute and homeless if he left her for someone else.

She hated David, ever since he had mocked her for carrying baby weight after the birth of their son fifteen years ago, publicly, of course, at a works function surrounded by female executive stick insects. She'd been breastfeeding at the time and had not wanted to leave Jake anyway, but he had insisted so she'd had to express through painful enlarged breasts and explain to her mother-in-law all about colic and how he might not settle. By the time she'd arrived at the party Cilla felt anxious that Jake's next feed was due and that David's mother hardly knew the child she was looking after. "He's a grazer," she'd said several times. "He has to get his wind up in between or he'll be sick." David was both sarcastic and rolled his eyes, after he had asked her if she had anything else to wear.

It was no wonder that things went downhill in their marriage after that night.

He made it abundantly clear that there were far more attractive women out there that he found far more interesting than Cilla. She ended up trapped in a corner with an old dear that was half deaf and talked about his pending hip replacement.

When she looked back this was not only the beginning of the end, but also the beginning of the bingeing that had made her balloon in size ever since. David had robbed her of her self-worth and as a result she had robbed herself of her health and her looks. She felt unattractive and so created it, and she knew that he was sniffing around younger bits of skirt to employ as his 'assistant' but she also knew that there was more to it than that. He'd been very shifty recently, and a couple of times, when she had brought him a coffee or a Scotch, he'd shuffled up the papers he was studying, as if to hide their contents.

Something was afoot and she knew it, and given half the chance she would love to take him down.

*Karma has a long memory David, and so does your wife,* she thought, as she opened a bag of toffee popcorn and a can of soda.

## Chapter 25

Millie awoke early and stretched in her bed.

*Hey.*

*Hey you.*

*I'm awake now, you can get some sleep.*

*Ok, I'll grab a couple of hours, got loads to tell you.*

*David Hill?*

*Yeah. Keep tabs on him and his wife Cilla will you?*

*Are you saying it's ok to think about another guy while I shower?*

*Just this once.*

*Ok, see you at school.*

*Laterz.*

Orin ran up to Millie on the driveway and linked her arm.

"Anything to report?"

"Just that they hate each other's guts and he wants to recruit a PA that gets very personal."

"Nothing new then," Orin said and shouted, "Hey!" as Blue jogged up.

"What's up?" he asked and Orin started to tell them what he had found out so far.

"I'll tell Emma when I catch up with her," Blue said. "And by the way, when I looked, David Hill seems to have a whole load of stuff coming his way from his wife."

"What kind of stuff?" said Millie.

"She's mad at him and she wants to tear him down, and she's going to get the chance any day soon."

"Are we clear to meet at lunchtime?" asked Orin, and Blue quickly checked.

"Yeah, see you then."

The morning dragged for Millie with the odd comment here and there from Orin about David Hill, and a full rundown on what his wife Cilla had from the all you can eat breakfast buffet place in the mall.

She held Orin's hand as they made their way to the forest clearing that had become a regular meeting place, and they stopped to kiss while they were alone.

*I love you.*

*I hope so.*

*Orin I do, please believe me.*

Millie looked at him with her hands cupping his face and she spoke out loud.

"I love you Orin."

"I love you too Millie, I really do."

They turned to walk further down the track and Orin couldn't hide the thoughts that galloped through his mind.

*But you might not choose me.*

Millie squeezed his hand and blinked back tears, she hoped she would never have to make such a choice, because even where love was concerned, she knew through experience that there were no guarantees.

"Hey!" said Emma as they approached, which meant *we're not alone Blue, cool it off!*

"Hey!" said Millie and they all sat on the fallen logs around the ashes of the fire they had burned nights ago, and started to share what they knew.

"So how do you think we'll get him out of the distribution deal?" said Emma.

"It's got to be his wife." Millie said and Orin nodded.

"Totally, she hates his guts and she would love to be able to crucify him in court for adultery and walk away with a fortune."

"Watch his demise from the moral high ground?" said Emma.

"You got it," Orin said, and looked at Blue.

"So you said something about her?"

"Yeah, when I started to lock on to him and his future possibilities I saw his wife enraged and throwing loads of stuff at him to do with adultery, money, work and more. It was like she had gone crazy, like batshit crazy."

Emma smirked. "She must have rumbled him somehow."

"That's got to be it," said Orin. "She's our secret weapon here, but how can we make sure she loses it like that and goes for him?"

"What's her hot button?" asked Millie. "You know, what would really, really get under her skin and cause her to explode?"

"I think it has to be another woman," Emma said, "and money, it's usually about sex and money."

"I think you are dead on," agreed Millie, "but how do we make sure she finds out about what he's been up to?"

Emma shrugged.

"I could go back in and make some little changes, set up a domino that would get him caught out..." started Millie and Orin butted in without letting her finish.

"You're not going back in there Millie."

"Just quickly, I mean it would be super easy and I could just..."

"No way." His tone was serious and she knew better than to try and persuade him any further. "I won't have you in that sort of danger again. There has to be another way."

"I could apply to be his new assistant!" said Emma. "And wait a few days until I have the chance to expose him, obviously not literally, oh God, stop talking Emma!" She blushed and Blue laughed at her, throwing an arm around her shoulders and tickling her.

"It would take too long," said Orin. "And he might not pick you, he wants someone with no intelligence remember."

"Oh yeah, but I didn't think that through so maybe I am actually perfect for the role..." Emma laughed again.

"Let's think about it, all we need to do is to make sure his wife gets to see all of the stuff he is planning. Now how can we do that?" Orin said.

"I think I've got it." Millie turned to him.

"Where is all of the information stored, like all of the yacht pictures and quotes, all of the job applications and inappropriate dialogue, all of the Compound X stuff and the Well Water plan?"

"It's on his laptop but it's highly encrypted and protected, there is no way anyone could read it."

"Without the passwords?" asked Millie.

"Yeah, and there will be several."

"But doesn't he think them out as he's typing them?"

Orin looked at her and a smile started to spread on his face.

"Of course he does Millie, you're a genius," and then he kissed her full on the mouth and got to his feet.

"Are you still friends with that geek, Simon?" he asked Blue.

"The hacker? Yeah, I still know him." Blue smiled too now, you didn't have to be a telepath to know what was coming next.

"You get his passwords, Simon hacks in and we what...?"

"Print it all out and send it special delivery to Cilla, it's about time she was in the picture," Orin shrugged. "My grandmother always used to say you should never start a fire you can't put out, well I have a feeling that David Hill's ideas for fanning the flames of desire are about to roar into an inferno that he's not expecting."

## Chapter 26

"Did you post it?"

"Yes," said Millie.

"Has it changed anything?" She turned to Blue.

"Oh my God!" he said slowly and deliberately and Millie felt her heart flip in her chest.

"What? What?" Orin shook him when he didn't answer straight away and Emma looked like she might cry.

"We need to get the news, he's reading a headline this afternoon and it's changing everything..."

"What's the headline? What's it changing?" Orin was starting to sound frantic, they had been making such good progress there was no way it could all go shits up.

"I don't know exactly, give me a chance man, back off." Blue pushed Orin to one side and leaned against a wall, steadying himself against the gravity of what he was seeing.

"There are suddenly loads of possibilities now, loads. It's like a whole can of worms has been opened and there are loads and loads of options flying around, but it all comes back to one event and that's the headline."

They waited, looking from one to another in terror and knowing that Blue was doing his best but wished he would hurry and drop the bombshell.

"Colin Hammond of Magnapharma Shot Dead by Cold Blooded Killer."

Emma burst into tears and Millie stared, open-mouthed. Orin started to pace and Blue just stood and shook his head.

"Holy crap," he said. "This could be the beginning of the end."

"Orin, can you hear him? Has it happened yet?" asked Millie, fighting back tears herself. "What have we done?"

"I'm trying, wait a second." He ran his fingers through his hair and focused. "Nothing."

"Let me try." Millie took a deep breath and closed her eyes. When she opened them the tears that gathered in the lower lids streaked her face. "Nothing, apart from his wife wailing and shouting that there has been a mistake."

"What the hell happened?" Emma's color had drained and she looked like she might be sick.

"I don't know," said Blue. "But I know that David Hill is going to read that headline and it's all going to blow wide open."

"He'll think it was to do with Compound X," said Emma.

"It probably was," said Orin. "We might never know."

"Unless I go and look," said Millie, and Orin started to object.

"What choice do we have now?" she spoke through her tears. "A man is DEAD Orin, DEAD. And it's going to blow this whole thing wide open! We have no idea what could happen next, Blue said it's all over the place, it's exploded. We've got no control now, and no choice. I have to go back in."

"No Millie, no, I can't let you..." Orin started to choke back tears now and he held her close. "I'm scared that something will happen to you."

"I know you are, I'm scared too but this is why I came here. I have to do this."

"Blue, what do you see?" Orin asked, trying not to allow the desperation in his voice to show.

"I see the same as before, a million outcomes."

"I have to do this," Millie said. "And I'll be back. I choose you Orin."

And with that he pulled her even closer and she felt his tears falling onto her cheek.

## Chapter 27

"Millie, be really clear about what you are doing and be as quick as you can." Orin spoke softly and kissed her forehead.

"I will, I just need to find Colin Hammond and work out what went so badly wrong, fix what I can and not set up any crazy dominoes."

"Correct. But you forgot that you are going to come back safely."

"I did, and I promise I will."

*I choose you, Orin, even if he's there, I choose you.*

*I love you.*

*I know, I won't be away long, you'll not even miss me.*

*Just come back safely.*

As Orin reached to tuck Millie's hair behind her ear, she closed her eyes and prayed that she would feel him touching her many times in the future.

She thought *Pause* and the scene around her froze into the statue-still frame that she fully expected. She could hear her own breathing and felt her heart beating hard in her rib cage, she knew that no matter how she had tried to hide her fear from Orin that he knew, knew she was as terrified as him about what could happen next.

*Rewind.*

As Millie thought his name, the Matrix reorganized to filter the layers that included Colin Hammond's energy. Iridescent stills stacked up at the front of her vision and then separated into segments, rather like the chapters of a living picture book. She was soon observing the happenings in Hazelwood Hall, and then stayed locked into the sequence of events as he traveled home with his wife and friends. They'd had to stop once on the journey for him to move from the back to the front seat, and in between he had a cigarette with a hand that still trembled slightly.

Once home he had poured a stiff drink and tried to pull himself together as his wife flustered and fussed around him plumping pillows. Eventually she had gone to bed and he had found himself alone, alone that is with the gripping fear of being haunted. The ghosts had said that he had to walk away from the Compound X project, or suffer the consequences, and he knew deep down that this project would wreck the lives of millions. If karma was real then it was payback time, and it was coming his way full force.

He had to bail out, or end up being terrified to within an inch of his life, or sectioned, or maybe both. He would have to forget about his plans, he had a good enough pension anyway and could increase his contributions. There was no way he could go through with it now, he was not the type to scare easy or even believe in all of the bullshit his wife did but this was different. They knew his name and what he was involved in, and that knife could have slit his throat. A deal too far, in too deep, however you wanted to spin the circumstances, he was screwed. He would have to email Alex tomorrow and tell him he was out, and that he'd have to find someone else to pick up the baton.

Millie watched him drink more and more until the shaking stopped and a numbness started to descend over him, as he dozed off to sleep.

*Forward.*

The next morning arrived with a headache for Colin both literally and metaphorically, as he swallowed two Advil and thought about how he was going to get out of the situation.

Alex was not a man to be messed with and Colin had been accepted into the circle of trust where the rewards were sky high. He was one of the chosen few, and to bail out at the very last minute was not going to look good. He didn't know who he was more scared of, Alex and how he might react, or the thought of the living dead coming back to warn him off.

He felt sick. Anxiety mixed itself up with his hangover and made him want to vomit.

*That was this morning...* Millie thought, this could get confusing and she needed a reference point to anchor her in the here and now.

*Forward.*

Colin was in the elevator at Humanetics HQ, fiddling with his tie in the mirror and sweating. Alex was expecting him, and he had been reading him since Colin stopped at McDonald's for a black coffee twenty minutes ago. The exchange was far better than Colin expected, and as they shook hands and agreed to part company he even joked that he'd been worried about breaking off the deal this late in the game.

"No worries," said Alex, it's all good. I know that it's not for everyone.

Relieved, Colin made his way back to the car park and thought about taking the afternoon off, his hangover was really kicking in now and the adrenalin and nervous tension that had been fueling him all morning was now starting to wear off and he was really feeling the come down. Nothing wrong with having the odd afternoon on the sofa when you were the boss, it was one of the perks.

He had no idea he was being followed, and the black Mercedes drove straight past his house as he pulled into the driveway, fuzzy headed and craving carbs. The tall hedge around the detached house meant that Alex could ask the driver to pull up without being noticed, and they waited. It was a nice neighborhood, and quiet so he wouldn't need to shift anything back if he was straight in and out.

Colin heard the doorbell and cursed, he wasn't expecting anyone and couldn't be bothered to answer it. Then it rang again and he reluctantly got to his feet and opened it.

"Alex, what can I do for you?"

"Oh I forgot to get you to sign a final non-disclosure statement to tie up all of the loose ends," he said and Colin saw he was carrying a black case.

"No worries, erm, come in." Colin led the way back to the front room but before he could offer Alex a seat he felt an almighty blow between his shoulder blades that knocked him to his knees, then flat on the floor.

A red hot searing pain accelerated through each nerve and fiber, faster than an instant. Colin gasped for air, but it came in short, punchy breaths and he could feel warm liquid pooling around him as his heart pumped out deep red blood onto the expensive marble floor.

"Drive," said Alex as he got into the back seat. "Oh, and we were never here."

"Understood, Boss." said the driver and hit the gas.

Millie looked around the murder scene and noticed a clock on the mantelpiece, 2:25pm, just a couple of hours ago. She should go back now to 4:15pm and tell the others what she had seen, then they could hatch a plan for her to shift it all back again.

She was shaken and needed to compose herself, and truth be known she felt partly responsible.

Maybe she should quickly look at Cilla's reaction to the mail, then she would have more or less the full picture to report back. God knows she didn't want to hang around but she didn't want to come back either.

Millie took a breath to compose herself as the image of Colin blurred and Mindy's thoughts and feelings filled her senses.

*Forward.*

David had left for work and Cilla was pottering around the kitchen when the mail fell on the mat, she shuffled over to get it and steadied herself on a sturdy oak sideboard as bent down to scoop up the pile of

letters. Huffing and puffing her way back to the countertop she sorted
it into his, hers, and recycling and flicked on the kettle.

"Biscuits..." she muttered and reached right to the back of the
cupboard and found a packet of double chocolate cookies.

Millie willed her to open the envelope that Orin had addressed, and
two cookies later she picked it up and started to analyze the
handwriting, all the while thinking *I wonder what's in here...*

*Just open it and you'll see!*

Millie screamed inside her head, she only wanted a quick idea of
what might play out and then she was gone. Cilla ran a nail file along
the seal of the A4-sized brown envelope and slid the contents onto her
lap. Her mouth fell agape and the end of the dunked cookie sludged to
the bottom of her coffee cup. Millie was expecting her to cry, or start
to smash things up as she flicked through the email correspondence
and applications that mentioned bra size, marital status and adult
interests.    She thought that Cilla's temper would erupt when she saw
the share certificates that had been transferred with forged signatures
and the suggested travel schedule from 'exclusive yachting holidays'.
Instead of sneering, the corners of Cilla's mouth started to turn up
into a smile, then a grin along with a full-on belly laugh.

*Got you, you SUCKER!*

She reached for the phone and gleefully dialed the offices of the
best divorce lawyer in town, and as she was holding and chuckling to
herself, she kept reading.

The line went dead as Cilla disconnected the call.

She continued to read and started the confidential dossiers on
Compound X, worldwide distribution plans and the manipulation of
humanity. She shook her head and read it again. This was the stuff of
Hollywood movies, and of nightmares. Surely he couldn't be

involved in something so evil? She took a deep breath and knew what she had to do next, she picked up the phone again and dialed out.

"CNN good afternoon, how many I direct your call?"

"Newsroom please."

"What is it regarding ma'am?"

"Something of global concern."

Millie's blood ran cold.

The possibilities were endless.

As the thought formed in her mind, a cascade of emotions, images, sounds and information started to layer and stack up in her awareness.

*These are just possibilities, get a grip of yourself.*

She thought as images of fear and rioting, death and destruction, elitism, mind control and more reeled across her perception like a non-stop 4-D movie. Millie choked back tears and tried to rationalize that none of this had happened yet, it could all be undone and that all she had to do was get back to the now and the others would help undo this mess.

The sounds of the screams were harrowing. Gunfire blazed through the Matrix as Millie covered her ears, the information was downloading so quickly that she doubted she could pause it even for a short reprieve, her emotional overwhelm had drained her of focus and energy and she could no longer contain her heart wrenching sobs.

Then silence. Apart from her own crying, and everything froze.

Millie looked up, wide-eyed and fearful still, spinning around in confusion.

"Millie." He spoke and her instinct was to run.

But run where? This was the endless fabric of time and space and they were together here in a split second freeze-frame between realities that in essence only existed to them, right now.

"Look at what you've done," he said as he approached her.

"I, I didn't mean it, I didn't do anything, it's just all gone wrong..." she stammered and stepped backwards. The space between the frozen images of what could become life on Earth expanded a little, allowing a uniform gap between her and the possibilities that hung around them both.

"It started with you Millie, you know that." Alex didn't sound sinister or upset, if anything he sounded amused. "It started when you came here, you were always the domino that would start this chain of events."

"You know nothing about me!" she objected and started to search through the suspended images mentally and frantically, where was the anchor that she had wanted to return back to?

"Is this who you're looking for?" asked Alex and drew closer an image of Orin and Blue sitting around the campfire talking in hushed tones.

*Play.*

She heard him think and the image came to life.

"You have to tell her," said Blue and Orin put his head in his hands.

"How can I tell her that? It's going to break her heart," he sighed.

"And it's going to jeopardize everything we've worked for," Blue said, and stared into the flames.

"It'll kill her if I tell her, I promised." Orin shook his head and Millie could feel that he was torn.

"You can't always keep your promise though, things change. You had no idea it would go this way, she has to understand that, it's not like you tricked her."

"But will she understand?" Orin looked at his friend now and Millie saw tears in his eyes.

"I don't honestly know at the moment, there are different possibilities depending on when you tell her and how."

"How can I tell her that I can't bring her mom back, Blue? It's going to rip her heart out and tear us apart too."

"You have to tell her the truth, that we tapped into the future possibility and that it was going to set up the biggest domino ever. She wouldn't even be here! You know that Orin, you know that her Walk In happened because her life was so shitty her soul was crying out for help.

Without that there would have been no soul exchange, and the Millie that you know and love wouldn't exist. And neither would we, we both know what would happen."

The frame flickered in and out and Millie lost them for a moment, then it reset and the conversation continued.

"I might have loved her the way she was," Orin said

"You didn't know she existed Orin, none of us did. We only noticed her when she walked in and her vibration lifted to be like us.

"There has to be a way to bring her mom back," said Orin, running his fingers through his hair. "There just has to be."

"Well it's not by stopping the accident from happening Orin, without the trauma of her mom's death and the aftermath of her life with her dad's drinking, there's no Walk In and no Millie. Not as we know her anyway." The image flickered again and Blue's voice faded.

"When did this happen?" screamed Millie and started to draw in the scenes before and after the conversation to gain some sort of timeline.

"Does it matter?" said Alex. "No matter when it happened, he still lied to you."

"He wouldn't lie to me! He loves me!" Millie's eyes darted left and right and holographic pictures moved at lightning speed like the pages of a book being turned one after the other in fast sequence.

Millie caught her breath, here it was.

The moment he'd plugged into her thoughts as she had relived the day of her mother's death, and how he'd wept with her at the terror and grief-stricken ordeal she'd lived through. The moment that he'd promised not to cloak his thoughts from her and he'd sworn beyond all else that he would find a way for her to save her mom and bring her back.

After all of this was done. Then the killer.

It was later that night as she slept that he'd spoken to Blue alone, carefully cloaking his thoughts, and selectively cloaking them from here on in so that she couldn't know that he was keeping the truth from her, in case she bailed. The image kept flickering, maybe she couldn't draw it in properly because she was upset.

He had lied to her not once but all the way through, was he lying about loving her as well?

Were they all just keeping her sweet in order to keep her on task?

"Millie, I didn't want to hurt you but you left me no choice," said Alex and reached out to touch her shoulder. She spun around and he could see the pain flash in her eyes as she shouted at him, the universe and everything.

"I don't know what to believe anymore! It's all crap, all of this, bullshit! I hate this whole stupid game of whatever it is, I just want to go back to being me!"

"Hey, come on, we can fix this." His voice sounded kind, and as he held out his arms Millie's instinct was to let him fold them around her. She cried with her head on his shoulder and he stroked her hair.

"I don't know who I am anymore," she whimpered.

"It's ok, I do." He spoke softly to her and she relaxed in his embrace, it felt like they were the only people in the world and in some ways they were.

"We can change this all around Millie, you and I would be invincible together," he continued.

"I don't want to be invincible, I just want to be loved." Alex kissed the crown of her head and held her tightly. "I know you do, and I have loved you forever."

"How could you possibly love me? You know nothing about me." Millie pulled away a little and looked at him.

"I know you far better than you think." As she closed her eyes and surrendered to his kiss, a feeling of déjà vu flooded over her. She had thought about this kiss many times since the last one, but never thought it would be under these circumstances. Guilt started to creep in and Orin's words echoed through her heart and mind, *choose me Millie, choose me.*

She pushed the thought away and kissed Alex back.

Orin had tricked her and lied, he didn't deserve her loyalty.

"But what are we going to do?" she asked breathlessly. "We can't just stay here in an imaginary bubble of a life forever, and after all is said and done, you want to rule the world."

"None of that matters now," he said, and Millie blinked and shook her head.

"What? You mean your master plan is shelved? I don't believe you." She laughed and he looked hurt.

"What if it was all to get us to this point?" He looked genuine, and Millie was confused.

"I don't get it," and a part of her didn't want to either as he kissed her again.

"I said I'd find you, I promised." He ran his fingers through her hair and familiarity tugged at her awareness.

"What, you mean after the restaurant?" she murmured.

"No, before."

"Before when?" Millie was lost in the moment and didn't want to talk. If the end of the world was imminent and her so called boyfriend had been deceiving her for weeks, she'd rather savor one moment to remember.

"Before we came," Alex said as he kissed the smooth, sweet-smelling skin behind her ear.

"You're talking in riddles," Millie said, tilting her head slightly as his lips moved down her neck to her collarbone.

"You haven't worked it out yet?" he asked and pulled back a little to look at her, quizzically.

"What are you talking about?" Millie asked and stood on her tiptoes to kiss his lips.

"Millie, you really don't know?"

"Alex, I have no idea what you are talking about, and quite honestly I don't think I care. I just want to be in the moment with you, before this all goes horribly wrong or I get a chance to shift it all back."

"And bring your mom back." He saw her shrink as he mentioned her mother, and he drew her close again. "I'm sorry, I really am. You're right, Millie, we can clean this whole mess up and bring your mom back as well. Together we can, I know it."

"I don't know Alex. I mean, maybe what Orin said was right, perhaps there is no way of bringing her back without undoing my Walk In. Maybe it's me or my mom, or the old me and my mom, it's just all so confusing and there is no way of knowing what kind of domino we could set up."

"But if we do that, we can undo them Millie, we can shift things around and then shift them back, you know that."

"But there has to be an end to what we can do, we aren't the masters of the universe that can keep commanding that the world dances to our tune, there has to be some kind of cut off, we're messing with nature."

"There has to be a way to keep you here and bring your mom back, I just haven't thought of it yet," he said, and looked her straight in the eye. "I promise."

"If you don't mind, I'm not falling for that again," Millie said. "I'd rather rely on myself if it's all the same with you, and I hate to rain on your parade but I can trump you any day on superpowers."

"You're just as feisty as you've always been," he chuckled.

"What are you on about? You're talking like we have some kind of history. I hardly know you... but I wouldn't mind getting to know you," Millie said.

"Well get to know me better," Alex said, and locked on to an image that lay buried in the array of options that surrounded them.

"That's your place?" Millie asked, trying to sound nonchalant.

"Yeah," said Alex cautiously. "Do you want to hang out?"

"Well, I erm..." Millie wanted to but an intuitive niggle was telling her this was wrong.

She looked at the roaring fire and champagne on ice and the image drew closer.

As she aligned with what it would feel like to sink bare feet into the sumptuous fur rug, she closed her eyes and he kissed her again.

"We can always come back here if you really want to and save humanity later," Alex said. "Let's just be together for a little while."

Millie didn't have to say another word, as soon as she agreed in her mind, the scene unfolded, candlelight flickered and the heady smell of roses filled the air.

"This is some place." She looked around at the contrast between old and new in the loft style apartment.

Stripped wooden floors and an original fireplace hinted at the history that the building was steeped in, clean lines and modern technology made it comfortable and modern.

The ceiling height gave more than enough space for an extravagant mezzanine, and Millie could see that this was where he slept.

He handed her a glass of champagne and her first reaction was to say no, which he read and smiled at her.

"Just enjoy the moment Millie, you've effectively paused reality for now so we can spend as much time as we want to together. You can go back to your friends at any point, if you want to that is."

"What if I don't want to?" she asked, sipping and allowing the bubbles to tickle her tongue.

"We have to go back and start reality eventually!" Alex laughed. "We can't leave the world frozen in time forever. Anyway, there's some kind of reset or default process that would happen if we did, I don't know a lot about it but I think there would be a point where things would start up again no matter what we did, I mean we're not God."

"You believe in God?" Millie asked, starting to relax a little.

Alex filled her glass halfway, and as the bubbles settled to make room for a top-up, he looked thoughtful.

"I don't know Millie, I think there's something. I don't know if it's the human idea of God but I know there's a creator or a creative energy that links everything, I mean how did it all come about? There has to be something."

"I agree, I'm not sure what it is but I know that we must come from somewhere and I know that we go back somewhere... at least I hope so." She swallowed the lump in her throat with another gulp of champagne and the familiar feeling of grief ebbed at the edge of her emotions.

"We'll bring her back, I promise. Can you imagine what we can do together?" He reached out and touched her cheek, his thumb brushed away a tear and he spoke again. "We can go back and put right all of the stuff that we need to and then we can look at the best way to bring your mom back Millie, and that will undo all of the crap your dad has gone through... we can right what went wrong and create a whole new reality."

Millie's eyes blinked back more tears and she spoke from her heart.

"I want to believe you."

"Believe me." He sounded sincere but it didn't stack up.

"Alex, I want to, I really do." She felt a little lightheaded and hot. "It's just that I don't know how you can be so different, I mean, I saw you kill a man."

"Colin Hammond?" he raised an eyebrow.

"I saw you shoot him and I know that you've been wanting to screw over humanity with your Compound X, how on Earth can I believe that you're all love and light now? And another thing, I can't believe that I have fallen for such a bastard."

"Nice guys finish last, Millie, it's always the bad boy that the girls fall for..."

"I'm only playing along with this because I know I can undo it," she said, and he laughed.

"So you are using me?"

"Yeah, kind of. I guess I am."

"It's my intention to go back and change what happened to Colin when we do the big cosmic clear up, it always was. I knew all along that whatever played out, good, bad or indifferent could have been changed or reversed, I just wanted to see what it would all play out like."

"You mean it's been a game to you?" she said, and shook her head.

"Kind of, but wait..." Millie had put down her glass and turned on her heel, he grabbed her elbow and as she spun around to look at him, "I did it for you," he said quietly.

Millie laughed out loud.

"For me?" she made an exaggerated gesture as her arm swept in a semicircle and her finger pointed back at herself. "For ME?"

"Yes, for you."

"This is getting crazier by the minute." She shook her head in disbelief and stumbled a little.

*No more alcohol.*

"I know, it's totally crazy, Millie. But I found you, and it's all played out the way that it should have."

"I don't get it. I've had too much champagne because none of this is making any sense to me at all. Maybe I should just sleep it off and we can go over this tomorrow?"

*Or I could wake up in a couple of hours and start undoing the fact that this ever happened.*

"It had to happen this way," he mumbled and something that felt like sadness radiated through him and into Millie's awareness.

She sighed, what on Earth was going on here?

She needed some space, some air but who knows how she would handle stairs or an elevator right now.

"Can I go to the bathroom?" she asked.

"Sure."

She locked the door and went to the large sash window that overlooked the street. A cool breeze wafted her way and the striped roman blind rattled against the wooden frame. She took a deep breath and gazed at the stillness of the world below, it was deadly silent and the streetlights cast an eerie orange glow onto the road and sidewalk.

Then a flicker, hardly anything, but something caught her eye.

A black cat slinked its way around a garbage bin and then ran off into the night.

*Oh no,* she thought then.

*Cloak.*

How could this be possible?

She had frozen everything in time and space, and that included cats.

She could feel panic rising as she looked around her, realizing that she had no idea where she was, never mind *when* this was, and what if the Matrix had restarted and all of those horrible things had happened? This could be months or years from then and the world outside of this apartment could be wracked with destruction. She could be sitting pretty with Alex and all of his millions in a luxury penthouse, God knows where.

*Don't panic, you can go back and change it.*

She tried to control her breathing, and went to the sink to splash cold water on her face.

*He'll be wondering what's taking you so long.*

The sound of footsteps made her jump, but not from outside the door, from the street below.

Millie dashed to the window to see a figure in a hooded jacket scurrying away, the pale face looked up at her for a split second and she was sure she saw something of a smile, as a small, white folded note swirled its way across the road and onto the window ledge.

She recognized the handwriting straight away and her heart started to race.

*Millie, we don't have much time now so you have to sober up and think fast.*

*From what we understand all hell was about to break loose just after you went looking to see what happened to Colin Hammond. David Hill's wife contacted the press about Compound X. It was somehow leaked on the Internet and went viral before the news report aired, and panic broke out on a global scale.*

*We think you paused reality just before this happened... but then somehow you ended up months in the future and time started to turn again.*

*Orin thinks it could be because you have had alcohol or maybe even Compound X, he says something has weakened your hold as a Shifter and that it's undone the pause, if you see what I mean. Anyway, I might not be explaining this very well, but we only just managed to find you a couple of hours ago and I've had to be quick.*

*We need you out of there and we need to work out how to get back to the pause to buy us some time to think.*

*We know what one of the possibilities was because it's played out since you have been gone, and it's not pretty. You're dad went way off the rails when you disappeared, he's still with us but he needs you. We all do, you're the only one that can stop this before it's too late. Millie, it's nearly too late.*

*Do what you can to get back to us here and now, it's October 22nd and we are camped out two streets over in an old pizza shop called Mama Mia.*

*Or get us back to the pause.*

*You've got this Millie, we know you have.*

*Blue says there are only two outcomes here, and we're praying that you can create the right one.*

*We love you.*

*Emma xxx*

Millie clutched the note to her chest and cried.

Whether she could forgive Orin or not was irrelevant now, she had to think about what to do next. She slipped the note into her back pocket and tried to connect with Emma.

Nothing happened.

*Closer.*

She tried but nothing.

She'd have to wait for a couple of hours, and she'd have to go back into the apartment.

"I was getting worried about you," Alex said, and passed her another glass of champagne.

Millie raised the glass as if to sip but the cold liquid merely wet her lips.

"I feel a bit funny," she said.

"Do you want to lie down?" he asked.

"Yes, maybe that's a good idea."

He took her glass and led her up the wrought iron spiral staircase that snaked its way up to the second floor. Millie slipped off her sneakers and curled up on top of the comforter. She wished that the room might stop spinning anytime soon and she'd be able to make sense of this.

How could she have been so stupid?

There was nothing she could do until she'd sobered up, so reluctantly she allowed sleep to descend. As she drifted into the halfway place between awareness and dreaming, she felt him next to her wrapping himself around her body and her first thought was *Safe.*

"I love you," she heard him whisper, and she felt his lips on the back of her neck.

"I promised I'd find you and I did."

"What do you mean you promised?" She spoke slowly and the words were punctuated with her slow, steady breath, her eyelids had fluttered closed.

"You still don't know? I love that."

She could feel the heat from his bare chest through the back of her t-shirt, one hand rested on her stomach and her head nestled in the crook of his elbow.

"That means that you might like me without the obligation."

"I don't get it."

"Wow, that pool of forgetfulness must have rinsed out your brain!" He chuckled and nuzzled her hair.

"Huh?" said Millie half half-heartedly. "You talk in riddles."

"It's worth it to be able to lie here with you in a real body, and to touch you and kiss you and hold you Millie. I know you are probably asleep now and you might not even be able to hear me, but a part of you will. You'll know, so I'll tell you anyway."

He stroked her hair lightly and Millie stirred a little.

"We both agreed to come to Earth at around the same time, I think you were a few weeks ahead of me. I couldn't tell you who I'd chosen, and you couldn't tell me either but we knew we'd find each other. I didn't recognize you at first, there was a feeling of something familiar and an attraction that I couldn't get out of my head, but we were on different sides…"

He took a breath and sighed it out.

"I can't explain the feeling that I had when I first saw you in physical form, it was weird and amazing. I knew it was you, you *feel* like you but with an extra dimension, it's hard to describe."

"I never wanted to cross swords with you, and I always knew that I would go back and undo all of the evil, but it was part of what had to happen. I just felt compelled to keep playing full out, like it was always meant to be this way."

A car drove up the street and Alex turned his head to catch the sound.

"It's time now," he said, and kissed her forehead.

"I love you and I always will."

"I love you," she said in her sleep and he hoped it was him she was dreaming of.

The world was awake now and the moment had arrived to complete his mission.

He stood over Millie and allowed his senses to drink her in one more time, knowing that whatever happened next she would always be his twin flame and hold his heart in the palm of her hand.

He scooped her up carefully and walked slowly, her arms locked behind his neck as he navigated the staircase and he laid her on the sofa.

The firelight highlighted her beauty and he felt a wave of emotion, probably gratitude, fill him from inside.

He covered her with a blanket and a dog barked in the distance.

*Uncloak.*

Hopefully Blue had seen that a part of the 'good' outcome had started with them talking.

*Hey, Blue?*

"Ok, he's made contact."

Orin stood up.

"Right, it starts here," he said, then thought *Uncloak.*

*She's fine, I wouldn't hurt her.*

*How do I know that?*

*You don't, you just have to believe me.*

*Why should I?*

*It's your only choice.*

*I can't hear her.*

*She's sleeping and dreaming, of one of us.*

*Has she had alcohol?*

*Yes, but not too much.*

*Enough.*

*Look, I had to.*

*What do you mean?*

*It was part of the contract, to get us to this place and undo what's been done.*

*So what now?*

*Now it's time to undo it all.*

*Not her Walk In!*

*No, not her Walk In, she's contracted to stay here for a whole lifetime now.*

*What about you?*

*You don't need to worry about me, ask Blue.*

"It looks like things could be coming good, at last. I don't have all of the details but it seems like we're in with a shot here." Emma hugged him tight and he hugged her back.

They turned again to Orin, waiting for him to tell them more as the conversation continued.

*I just want you to know that there's no hard feelings.*

*Whatever. It's not over yet.*

*It soon will be.*

Alex made his way back upstairs and looked down on Millie.

*Goodbye my love,* he thought, as he saw a spark from the fire leap onto the rug and smolder.

It didn't take long for the draft from the bathroom window to fan the spark into a flame and soon the rug was on fire and the flames licked the nearby table and armchair.

The smoke alarm started to sound and Millie stirred, confused and still sleepy, she rubbed her eyes awake and started to cough.

"Alex!" she screamed as she saw the fire. "Alex!"

The bottom of the blanket that had cocooned her moments earlier was thrown across the room as the edge started to burn, and she stood up making her way towards the door.

By now the bottom of the wooden mezzanine was smoking and Alex could feel the heat rising along with the thick black smoke.

Millie saw him and shouted again, "Alex! Jump!"

He shook his head as the flames grew taller, and she could see tears in his eyes.

"I'll be waiting for you Millie, play full out and get Home safe."

"I don't know what you mean! Just jump please, even a broken leg is better than being cremated!"

"I have to go, I said I'd find you and I'd help you so now the contract is complete. I love you."

"Stop talking in riddles and jump!"

"This is Alex Jackson checking out, or AJ to you, Millie. I'll watch over you, and we'll be back together soon. Time passes much more quickly at Home but to you it will seem like a lifetime."

Realization hit her like a truck and she fell to her knees.

"AJ, no! I didn't know it was you, please don't go!" she screamed above the sound of the flames and destruction and became aware of people banging on the door and shouting.

Millie curled up and sobbed, the fire may as well take her too, she couldn't save the world now or herself.

*Millie.*

*Orin?*

*Thank God, Millie can you hear me?*

*Yes, barely, I'm slipping Orin, I can't breathe so well.*

*You're going to get out of there, Millie, we're coming for you, we are so close.*

*I don't know if I can hang on Orin, it's an inferno.*

227

The sound of sirens getting closer and people on the street below faded in and out.

Millie looked up at the flames and thought about their beauty, as they wrapped around the beams above her. Searing heat filled the room and she prepared herself for the end.

Before she lost consciousness she looked up once more, and as the mezzanine burned ferociously, there seemed to be a split second where the image froze, flickered and then resumed. It looked like there was a faint slit of light visible for a moment, but it could have been a memory or imagination, as her heart and soul surrendered.

*This is it,* she thought, and started to drift.

## Chapter 28

"Millie! Millie!" Oh God, will she be ok?"

"Stand back please, we need to get her to hospital as soon as possible."

An oxygen mask was slipped over her face and she was strapped to the stretcher before the ambulance started its engine and its siren.

"I've got to come with her!"

"Ok, ma'am, just stay calm, please buckle up."

## Chapter 29

"Hey."

Millie sat up in her hospital bed and smiled broadly.

She knew they were coming of course, she and Orin had been talking nonstop since she'd regained consciousness.

The three of them sat around her bed and looked at her.

"How are you feeling?" Emma broke the silence.

"Oh, okay I guess, they said I can come out tomorrow." Millie took Orin's hand and he smiled at her.

*Are we good?*

*Of course.*

*Good.*

"So what's new in the world?" Millie asked, as a nurse plumped her pillows then left the room again.

"Where do we start?" said Emma.

"I've told her some stuff," Orin confirmed, "but not all of it, I didn't want to overload her too early."

"I'm fine!" said Millie. "Now tell be everything!"

"You have to understand that our version might be different to yours though," said Emma.

"Remember when you set off the fireworks and then you went back again and undid it? We thought nothing had happened right? Because reality stopped, changed and then resumed. So for other people that's the way it has always been... weird, I know. A Shifter knows the before as well as the after, but the rest of us don't."

"Right, so if you tell me what you think happened and I'll fill in the blanks. Deal?"

Emma talked for nearly an hour about the light and dark battle, and how they thought that Millie might choose Alex and join the Dark Side.

They told her about the demise of Compound X.

The technology that was going to be used to create the energy vibrations that they needed to influence the changes in humans was all programmed into a series of microchips that were installed into a supercomputer. It was unfortunately compact enough for someone to steal when there was a burglary in the Humanetics Head Office. No one else would know what the intelligence was for, so it's likely that the machine had been discarded or was in some kid's bedroom running Minecraft.

It turned out that the time jump into the future had manifested as Millie going AWOL on Earth for a while, like she had simple disappeared for a couple of weeks without any contact.

There had been a campaign to find her and they had done everything they could to locate her and log in.

"We thought you were dead," Emma started to cry. "Everyone did, you just vanished and no one knew anything."

"Thank God we looked in the book," said Orin, squeezing her hand again.

"Yes, glitches. I'd never noticed them before but apparently they show up in the Matrix when something goes wrong or something is changed. It's like a scar in time and space, where reality has been chopped, expanded, influenced or stitched back together. It's the point where something has been altered." Emma sniffed and continued. "We realized that after you had paused there must have been a glitch and something had been altered. We knew then that he'd found you in the Matrix and he was somehow trying to cover his tracks or move things around."

*Alex.*

"It's ok," said Orin softly, "I know you had feelings for him."

*Had?*

"Millie, he's gone." Orin spoke quietly and they sat in silence.

She opened her mouth to apologize for the tears that came next and he kissed her forehead.

"No need to be sorry, you can't help who you love."

*I love you.*

*I know you do, and you loved him as well.*

*Thank you.*

*What for?*

*Understanding.*

*Love always understands.*

"I think I saw a glitch," Millie said. "What does it look like?"

"It's hard to describe, I guess it's like when your computer is going to crash and the screen freezes for a moment or flickers on and off for a second, then rights itself again," said Blue.

"And that means that something has been changed?" Millie asked.

"Yeah, like the original blueprint of what was going to happen naturally, the natural course of events if you like has been altered in some way. So if you see a glitch, a Shifter has been in and made a change, good or bad," explained Orin.

"Right," nodded Millie and thought about the conversation she had heard between Orin and Blue.

Orin looked at her strangely.

"Erm, that convo that you think we've had..." he pointed at Blue and then back at himself, "we haven't."

"But I thought that you said you couldn't risk undoing my Walk In and you wouldn't help me, I thought you'd lied to me."

"I've never lied. What did it look like, what was I saying?" Orin was being patient with her but she could feel he was hurt.

"You and Blue were sitting in the woods and you were talking about me, about how you desperately wanted to help me but you couldn't, and then it flickered in and out like you said."

"I don't remember that either Millie," said Blue. "But it sounds like a glitch to me, it's been created from a load of possibilities, altered or erased altogether. Like Emma said, a Shifter's version is different because you have overall awareness of what you've done, we don't.

We just experience life as it unfolds, and most people would never even notice the odd glitch. You have to have heightened awareness and know that they exist to see them."

"But I didn't change that or influence it or anything, I just saw it play out," Millie objected.

"It must have been Alex... but why would he do that? I don't get it."

"To make you think Orin wouldn't help you?" Emma said what the three others were thinking.

"Yes, probably that. He knew how much it meant to me and if Orin wasn't going to help me get her back that I'd go ahead anyway and risk it myself."

The three friends exchanged perplexed glances and Orin spoke up.

"Get who back Millie?"

She looked at him with her mouth agape and choked on her tears. "You know full well Orin, what the hell are you playing at?" she spat at him and he recoiled for a moment. As he heard her thoughts the door handle turned and in walked the lady in question.

"We had better let you rest," said Blue and they all stood up to go, making room for Millie's mom.

## Chapter 30

"I know what happened now," Millie said as they walked hand in hand towards school.

"Well how come I don't?" Orin tickled her ribs and she laughed.

"I just needed to work it out for myself that's all, get some headspace I guess."

"I'm just playing with you, I know it must be a total mind flip from what you've said."

"The biggest mind flip ever." Millie rolled her eyes.

"So are you gonna spill now? Or do I have to force it out of you?" He tickled her again and she squealed.

"Ok, ok, enough already!"

"Let's go somewhere we can talk." Orin said.

*We can talk anywhere.*

*I know that but I want to be with you when you tell me, and you have math now and I have biology.*

"Ok, you win. But what if we get caught?"

"I've already asked Blue and he says it's cool."

They sat in the cafe and huddled hot chocolate. As Millie stirred in marshmallows she told him about what she'd seen on the night of the fire.

"He must have gone back into the Matrix then and changed something, because up until then I know that my mom was dead."

"But what could he have changed?"

"That's it, I only knew for sure when I overhead my parents talking last night. They were saying how much they loved me and that the fire was as bad as the car crash way back when I was a kid. I honestly can't remember that much about it but I do remember coming home from a hospital feeling weird. They said that they had had some kind of argument and mom was leaving and I'd got into the front seat to go with her. I hadn't had a seat belt on and we were in a collision. I went through the windscreen and was in pretty bad shape by all accounts."

"That must have been when you Walked In."

"Yeah, that's what I thought too, it's often at the point of injury, surgery, extreme trauma or whatever."

"And that's where he made the change, I got into the car. Because a part of me has a memory of not getting in and watching my mom driving away from my bedroom window. I was screaming the place down for her to turn around and come back."

"That will be part of the old version of you and cell memories and stuff."

"I guess."

"And another thing, I've got this scar on my forehead, like just recently but it looks and feels old."

Orin reached forward and moved her fringe to one side. "You've always had that Millie, since I met you you've had that scar," he said.

"Orin, I haven't, I just know I haven't. It's just appeared!"

"Really, it's always been there!" he tried to assure her.

"I'm going to look at some old photographs and see when it first appeared, I swear to you that it's new." Millie ran her index finger along the silvery line etched into her skin.

"Millie, it's been there since the day we met, on the first day of high school."

"You mean the broom cupboard, right?" she asked, and Orin looked vague.

"What are you talking about?" he said, looking confused.

"After I bolted from the science lab..." she said, "the day you were looking for me, remember?"

Orin shook his head.

"The day you first took me to meet the others in the forest and showed me the book and everything." Millie sounded exasperated, and then as the penny dropped she sighed and chuckled.

Orin shrugged. "Oh Boy, this is going to take some unraveling. You'd better get us another hot chocolate," she said and leaned over the table to kiss his forehead.

## Epilogue

Things had never been so good.

Last year had been a whirlwind on all levels, and seemingly no matter when she had met Orin, or what had happened since, he loved her and she loved him. Her mom and dad were getting along really well, and even though there were echoes of an alternative reality in her mind some days, they were fading and making way for the good times. It was her mom and dad's wedding anniversary and the weather had blessed their garden party with glorious sunshine. Glasses were raised and congratulations rang out. As Orin kissed her cheek, Millie wondered if things could stay this way forever.

*********

Miles away in a neighboring state, a diligent employee had stayed back to tidy the warehouse at Nutritech. He didn't know the man in the suit that had given him the bundle of notes, but suits came and went in big corporations and he didn't want to mess up. That Miles woman had given him a chance and he wasn't going to blow it. He needed his job and he'd do what he was told, especially when he was handed a roll of fifties.

He found the bottles sure enough, they were under lock and key just like he'd said. In a big steel container, shoved right at the back underneath shelves heaving with the weight of files containing who knows what. He dragged out the eight plastic bottles and took them, as he'd been told, outside and around the back of the building. There were no security cameras here. It certainly had no smell or color, it was ionized water just as the suit had said.

He tipped the bottles one by one into the slow flowing stream, disturbing the silt on the bottom and making brown mud clouds, as it wound its way to the reservoir. He had no idea why he had to do it this way, but as he threw the now empty bottles into the dumpster and made his way back to lock up, the suit nodded at him from across the car park.

That's the easiest 500 bucks I've made in my life, he thought, and lit up a cigarette as he padlocked the doors and made his way home.

## The End

## Acknowledgements

Thank you to life in general for your challenges and ongoing lessons. I am learning that the storm will pass and make way for new growth, even when it doesn't feel that way at the time.

To my daughter Amy, what did I do with my life before you came? I am eternally grateful that your soul chose me, my world turns for you and it always will.

To my precious niece Anna Eilbeck. You are one of the greatest gifts of this lifetime for me, and you are so, so loved.

Thank you to my inner circle. The people that know the real me and keep me going, prop me up and cheer me from the sidelines. The people on speed dial when I have a wobble. If you have a handful of these you are very blessed in life.

I include my husband Darren, my parents Pam & Graham and my sister Emma. They are my first port of call when life gets rough.

I am blessed with the friendship of some wonderful people who step in when they are needed. The ones I have needed recently are Jane Turner, Amanda Fletcher, Jennie Harrison, Anne Strojny, Anna Pereira, Jill Newton, Sheena Waters and Carrie Craig Gilby - thank you, you all know why you have had a mention.

I want to say a big business thank you to Emma Holmes & Claire Mitchell, they can deliver the greatest business insight with tough love when I need it, and always from a place of having my best interests at heart. You are both loyal friends and trusted colleagues.

You are both my compass when I lose direction and my anchor when the sea of life gets choppy. I could not have got this far without either of you pushing me forward past my own fears.

Love and gratitude to Matthew Reeves-Hairs thank you for being there at the drop of a hat if I need you and Jay Sykes, my wonderful media man.

And to the little people in my life. Harriet Turner, Jack Swinburn, Sam Swinburn, Katie Waters, Abby Waters and Lottie H. I love watching you all grow, you feel like family and I love you being around. I wanted to write something that you might want to read someday. Just so you'd know that I do more than just great sleepovers, sky lanterns and wooden spoon karaoke......

A huge thank you goes to the lovely Michelle Emerson. My sounding board, editor, typesetter and friend. Your work is always excellent and you take so much of the stress away from writing for me. I am so fortunate to work with you.

And finally thank you my Tribe. All of the visitors to my Facebook page, the blog and the book readers, my lovely club members and the people that buy my programs.

I am living my dream because of you, and I am hoping to continue serving you all for a very long time.

Love Kate x

**Also by Kate Spencer**

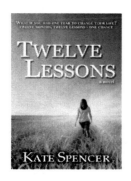

*(Contains Adult Content)*

\*\*\*

*Coming Soon…*

**Twelve Lessons Later**

**Connect with Kate Spencer**


www.facebook.com/thelightworkersacademy


instagram.com/lightworkers_academy


kate@thelightworkersacademy.com


**Work with Kate Spencer**


Kate has an online consciousness club and several online programs that are designed to help to grow, expand and enrich your life in amazing ways.


www.thelightworkersacademy.com